Breathless

CHARISSE C. CARR

Disclaimer

CHECK YOUR TRIGGERS

The character Wanda "Strawberry" Stevenson is unhinged. There is no limit to her craziness. She will do things some may find disturbing in this series. I don't want to give away any details or the plot twist, so enter at your risk. If you choose to continue on, buckle up and enjoy this wild ride! If this is your first read by me, prepare to be entertained and shocked at all the twists and turns.

Chapter One

MECCA HOLLAND

"Damn, this pussy good as hell. You 'bout to make me cum."

"Issa 'bout time. You know I gotta finish deliverin' these people mail. This was supposed to be a quickie, and yo ass tryna sleep in it. Hurry up," I complained, tossing my ass back even faster to help him out.

My husband, Major, currently had me bent over on some boxes in the back of my mail truck, dicking me down.

"Slow down before you break my shit." He tightened up the grip he had on my hips.

"Nah, nigga, you gotta plant them seeds now. The crack of my ass is sweatin'. It's hot as hell in here."

"Sssssss," he hissed.

When Major started sounding like air coming out of a tire, I knew he was about to bust. Slowing down, I allowed him to take back control. Major slammed into me three times before releasing his load.

"A'ight, pull out and let me up."

This man was acting like we weren't parked on a side street in the middle of the day and actually tried to relax on top of my back.

"Shit, I was just enjoyin' the moment. We barely have time to fuck and when we do, all you do is complain. Rushin' me, when all I wanna do is make you feel good."

Major wiped his dick off with the wipes I handed him, then tossed them in the little garbage can I kept in my truck.

"Well, I didn't, so there's that." I frowned. "And I'm on the clock. I need to be done by a certain time, so I can pick up the kids and head home to get dinner started. You will still be at work while I'm wrestlin' wit' three kids under five."

After I cleaned myself up, I fixed my clothes and started organizing the mail I was to deliver next.

"I'm sorry that spendin' time wit' cho husband is such a chore for you. I have a timeline to keep to as well, but I drove 'cross town to make sure I'm still takin' care of home. And to have you insult me, talkin' 'bout you didn't cum, doesn't help. See you lata."

Major exited out of the back of the mail truck and slammed it shut. He was pissed and had every right to be. Sometimes I didn't know when to shut my big ass mouth. When he called me earlier and said he wanted to meet up for a quickie I agreed because we both needed it.

Before he arrived, I received a phone call from the daycare center saying one of our twin girls decided to eat a glob paste. They said she was alright, but we should keep an eye out in case she fell ill later. So when Major showed up, that was at the forefront of my mind. It was my fault I didn't climax because mentally I was somewhere else.

The way I made him feel just now was fucked up. Major did everything he could to make me happy, especially when it came to sex. He knew how to make my body yearn for him, and I missed the way we used to be. When Major and I first met, we would fuck like rabbits all day long and didn't care where we were at. I started getting all warm inside as I thought back to one of our escapades.

"You sure no one is goin' to come in here?" I questioned Major as he led me to the storage room of a restaurant he used to work at.

We were sitting down, waiting for the waiter to bring out our drinks and appetizers, when he got the urge to sample me. When Major told me how he wanted to put me on the table and sit my ass on a plate in front of him, so he could suck all the juices out of my pussy, I was ready to do his ass right then and there.

"They only come in here at the end of the night when it's time to clean up and restock everything. Just don't be all loud and shit when I'm bustin' yo ass," he joked.

"Shit, you be the one moanin' and groanin', soundin' like someone stabbed you in the side wit' a dirty blade." We laughed.

The storage room was out of the way, toward the back of the restaurant and down this long, dark hallway.

When we got inside, Major put a chair under the doorknob to jam the door shut in case someone tried to open it. I sat my handbag down on one of the boxes.

Wasting no time, he pulled down the front of my off the shoulder maxi dress I had on. My titties were on full display as he pushed them together and viciously attacked each one. As he licked and sucked on my nipples, I freed his dick from the Nike basketball shorts he had on. It was a beautiful, summer day, therefore we were both casually dressed.

Major nibbled on my neck and squeezed my ass after letting his hands slide up my dress. I wasn't wearing any panties, so he had full access. When his fingers found their way to the slit in my pussy, I moaned out loud when he massaged my clit.

"Shhhhhh," he whispered in my ear.

"You make me feel so good," I murmured.

"Imma 'bout to make you feel even betta."

Next thing I knew, Major, who stood at five eleven and was 180 pounds of pure muscle, picked me up and rested my back up against the wall. He slid his manhood into my warm, wet, center, delivering stroke after stroke.

I wrapped my legs around his waist while our tongues wrestled for position as we passionately kissed. Squeezing my pussy muscles, my walls contracted around his big, black dick, causing Major to moan into my mouth.

"Damn, Mecca, that shit feels crazy."

His strokes became fast and furious. We stared into each other's eyes, reaching our peak at the same time.

"Sssssssss." Major released his load.

My legs shook as I buried my face in his neck.

"They probably out there lookin' for us." Major laughed.

When he put me down, I went into my handbag and got the baby wipes I kept in a baggie for moments like this. We cleaned up and removed the chair from the door. Major made sure the coast was clear before we headed back out to our seats.

"Where did y'all sneak off to?" the waiter quizzed when he returned back to our table, raising his eyebrows.

Major and I looked at each other and smiled.

Bang! Bang! Bang!

The sound of someone banging on the side of my mail truck startled me, bringing me out of my thoughts.

It was Mrs. Mabel mean, old ass. I slid the door open to talk to her. She was in her house robe, had a scarf around her neck, and sported a pair of rain boots on her feet. It was eighty degrees outside, so I know Mrs. Mabel was hot as hell.

"I saw a man leave up outta here. Y'all musta been in here hunchin' all ova the mail. Imma report cho ass if you don't got my check I've been waitin' on, heifer," she threatened.

Mrs. Mabel worked my nerves every damn month over a fifty dollar check she received from one of her kids.

"You betta mind yo business before I call the city and tell 'em 'bout the three monkeys you have livin' in yo house. It's illegal in the state of New Jersey to have certain wild animals as pets," I fired back.

"I'm Ray Charles and didn't see shit, bitch. Just fork ova my mail, so I can get back to the house before they tear my shit up, wit' cho funky ass," Mrs. Mabel mumbled.

She was too busy rushing out of the house to find me that

she forgot to put her teeth in. Mrs. Mabel lived over on the adjacent street.

"This has to stop. You do this bullshit every month. Yo block was next, so there was no need for you to come huntin' me down like this." I gathered up her mail. "Here!"

She was pissed that I shoved the letters in her hands.

"Mecca, don't make me fuck you up."

Mrs. Mabel stood there and looked through her mail until she found the one from her daughter. When she did, this lady held the letter up to her nose and sniffed it.

"Why are you smellin' the mail?" I quizzed.

"Makin' sure it don't smell like dussy?" Mrs. Mabel twisted up her lips.

"Dussy?"

"Yeah, dick and pussy." She stuck up her middle finger at me and walked off.

"That's why yo ugly ass look like Mrs. Avery from *The PJs,*" I yelled out my door before closing it.

Pulling off, I continued on my route, not letting her ruin my day. Once I was done, I went to pick up the kids and headed home.

* * *

"Come on. We got 'bout five minutes before they start lookin' for us." I pulled Major into the bathroom.

The kids were sitting on their bean bags in front of the TV watching *Spongebob*. It would only hold their attention for a short amount of time, but it would be long enough for me to apologize to my husband.

We barely said two words to each other when he got home from work. Once dinner was done, we ate together as a family but focused all our attention on the girls. Afterwards, I bathed them while he cleaned up the kitchen. It was our everyday routine.

We alternated roles each night. Major was definitely hands on when it came to our girls. The problem was by the time he got in from work to help, I had already been home with them alone for four hours. Trying to cook and clean with three kids wanting all your attention at the same time wasn't easy.

I tried putting the twins in a playpen together, but they would climb right on out. Even with the gates up, that kept them out of the kitchen, all three girls would stand at it crying, wanting me to pick them up. They have been clingy from birth, and it was all my fault. All I did was hold them and let them do whatever they wanted. It wasn't until I went back to work that I finally got into a regular routine with them.

"Why you lockin' us in the bathroom?" Major quizzed, looking confused.

"I wanna say sorry to my amazin' husband for not appreciatin' the effort he made to put us first today."

When I grabbed his dick through his pants, he allowed a grin to form on his face. After putting the lid down on the toilet, I took a seat as Major stood in front of me.

"Apology accepted." He stared down at me.

Unbuckling his pants and pulling down the zipper, I slid Major's pants and boxers to his knees. Knowing I only had minutes to make him cum, I wrapped my lips around the head of his brick hard dick and went to work.

I grabbed his ass and pushed him further into my mouth. Sucking and slurping like my life depended on it, I gave him sloppy head. It wasn't sensual, sexy, or pretty. All I could think about was the kids knocking on the door and calling our names, so I rushed it.

"Damn, you scraped my shit with yo teeth," Major informed me.

Feeling bad and not wanting to do it again, I replaced my mouth with my hands. When Major told me he was about to come, I put his dick back in my mouth just in time to catch and swallow.

As soon as we got ourselves together and exited the bathroom, the kids were makin' their way down the hallway, so we finished just in time.

"Thank you," Major whispered in my ear.

He patted me on the ass then picked up our oldest girl. The twins each grabbed one of my hands as we made our way back to the living room. I put on a movie, and we all relaxed together.

"Go get in the shower while I put 'em in the bed." Major rubbed the back of my neck once the movie ended.

"Okay, and I'll read 'em a story, so you can get in when I'm done."

While in the shower, I thought of how I missed Major

coming in to join me. The touch of his hands on my wet skin as the water rained down on us always gave my pussy a pulse. I threw my head back and rubbed on my titties, allowing my hands to find my sweet spot.

Thinking of him entering me from behind was turning me on. I grabbed my mini vibrator from out of the plastic soap dish container I kept it in. With my left leg resting on the ledge inside the shower, I pleasured myself until I gave my body the relief it needed.

Chapter Two

MAJOR HOLLAND

"Bruh, the shit is gettin' outta hand, and Mecca don't see nothin' wrong wit' it."

My brother, Savior, took a bite of his pizza and shook his head. We were currently parked by Seven Presidents Oceanfront Park. We met up for lunch today and decided to get pizza from Atillio's in Long Branch. Since we were little kids, that had been our spot. I was now thirty-five, and Savior was thirty-seven.

"Man, listen, you gotta put cho foot down. I love my sis-in-law, but she needs to chill wit' lettin' my nieces sleep wit' y'all every damn night."

I was venting to him about how after we settled down for bed last night and was about to get it in, the girls came out of their room and wanted to get in our bed. Instead of Mecca making them go back to their room, like we agreed, she allowed them to crawl in between us, once again.

This was one of the biggest obstacles in our marriage. We both worked, therefore our time alone was limited. I was a graphic designer for an advertising agency and had to put in long hours most days. When it was time for my head to hit the pillow at the end of the day, I wanted to rub on my wife's ass, not get kicked in the face and head all night by a three-year-old.

"I did, and she acted like I ain't say shit. It's to the point that I go and sleep in the livin' room. My back fucked now from the shit," I complained.

"Sienna was the same way wit' our kids. You know her and Mecca cut from the same damn cloth. They different but the same in so many ways." Savior blew his breath.

He was married to Mecca's twin sister. We met them ten years ago at a Summer Jam concert. They were identical in the physical but had their own style visually and personality wise.

My wife always kept her hair cut short, like Toni Braxton short, while Sienna had shoulder length hair. Sienna always dressed like she was about to do a photoshoot for a magazine. Mecca, on the other hand, loved the casual and relaxed fit.

"And how did y'all get past it or do they still pile in, dividin' and conquerin' shit?" I quizzed.

Savior and Sienna's kids were older than ours, so they already experienced what we were just going through, but my brother and I never had conversations like this before. The only reason I even mentioned anything to him was because it was starting to take a toll on me mentally.

I didn't have too many people I could confide in besides family, and our parents were my last resort. My dad would say I was acting like a bitch. He didn't believe in a man complaining or showing emotions. We also didn't have the best relationship.

My mom would automatically take Mecca's side without even hearing me out completely. I couldn't even finish my sentence before she would cut me off and start going in. She admired the fact that Mecca worked outside of the home and still managed to take care of home, therefore she could do no wrong in her eyes.

"Shit, we ended up in counselin'. It was either that or get a divorce."

Savior kept eating his food without a care in the world, like what he just said wasn't crazy as hell. This was the first time I heard about any serious issues in their marriage. Mecca couldn't have known because she definitely would have mentioned it to me.

"Ova the kids sleepin' in y'all bed, my nigga?"

"Nah, it's neva really 'bout the issue that started the argument. Everythin' you been thinkin' or feelin' shows up when you angry and start fussin'. You know that. We both said some shit we couldn't take back, and it went downhill from there," he explained.

"Why you neva said nothin' to me? I thought y'all had the perfect marriage and all along, y'all were hangin' on by a thread." I shook my head.

"Bruh, how do I come to you as a man and say my marriage 'bout to be ova wit'? I always told myself my kids will neva grow up in two different homes or hafta choose sides but in reality, they almost did. We both know how that feels. I don't want that for my kids or my nieces, so fix yo shit before history repeats itself."

Our parents got divorced when I was ten and Savior was twelve. Even though they never asked us to choose sides, it was expected. The judge gave our mom primary custody after asking us who we wanted to live with. We stayed with our dad every other weekend and during the summer.

He never cheated on our mom, but didn't respect her as a woman. She had to give up her career once she had us to become a stay-at-home wife, which she hated. All day long she catered to our needs while neglecting herself. Even as young kids, we saw how unhappy she was.

One day she packed us up and left. We stayed at our grandparents house until the divorce proceedings ended. Our mom was granted the family home and moved us back in once our dad moved out. He never forgave us for not choosing him.

"You come to me the same way I just came to you. And Mecca and I ain't gettin' no divorce, ever, but we damn sure need a third party to get involved before we be sleepin' in separate rooms permanently," I admitted.

We finished up our lunch and went our separate ways. He had his reasons for not telling what was going on in his marriage, and I had to respect it even if I didn't like it.

"How dare you darken my doorstep without those beautiful lil girls trailin' behind you?" My mother stared at me through the screen door.

"Ma, unlock it and let me in." I shook the handle for added effect.

"I'm serious. Where are my babies?" she questioned.

"I decided to stop here on my way home from work. I'll bring 'em by this weekend."

"You betta." She smiled and allowed me to enter my childhood home.

My mom lived alone and refused to downsize. There was no need for a single woman to maintain a four-bedroom, two-story home. We tried to get her to rent it out and get something smaller for herself, since selling it wasn't an option, but she refused.

"So, what's going on? Something must be heavy on yo heart for you to come by here before going straight home. It's already getting late." She glanced down at her watch.

My mother was always a straight shooter when it came to us. Once she left my father and found her voice again, she never held her tongue.

"I just wanted to check on you and see how you were doin', that's all. We don't get to many moments alone, and I need to do better when it comes to that."

After my lunch with Savior and finding out his marriage wasn't what I thought it was, I decided to pay my mom a visit.

"Bullshit! What the hell did you do to my Mecca?" she questioned while walking into the family room.

"Nothin', chill. You on go for no reason." I shook my head and sat across from her in the recliner.

This used to be my dad's favorite spot. When he came in from work, he dropped his things at the door then sat down and relaxed. My mom would bring him a cold drink after picking up his stuff. I wondered why she never threw it out.

"Imma fuck yo ass up if she calls and tells me otherwise. You know she's my favorite." My mom cut her eyes at me.

"You not supposed to have favorites, Ma."

"Boy, hush yo mouth. I can do what I want 'cause I'm grown. I love Sienna just the same, but Mecca reminds me so much of myself. The relationship I have with her is different, that's all," she defended.

"And that's what scares me." I mumbled, but she heard me.

The expression on my mom's face wasn't pleasant at all.

"What the fuck does that mean, Son?" She furrowed her brow.

"Mecca and I are goin' through a lil rough patch right now. As much as I try to reason wit' her, she just won't budge. I'm afraid that if I try and force her to do what I wanted from the very beginnin', she might take the kids and leave like you did."

I took a deep breath and waited for my mom to respond. When she sat up and pointed her finger toward my face, I regretted stopping by.

"Yo ass is more like yo father than you care to admit." She spoke through clenched teeth. "Y'all thought process is the same when it comes to how a home should run and gender roles. It's disgusting and makes me sick."

"Me and that nigga ain't the same. I don't treat Mecca like a slave and make her cater to my every need," I fired back, feeling offended.

"No, but that's what cho ass wanna do deep down inside. Mecca told me how you acted when she decided to return to work. I'm just glad she chose to do what was best for her 'cause you men forget that we are women first. Bein' a wife and a mother doesn't define who we are. Y'all couldn't walk a day in our shoes but are always trying to tell us which ones to put on. What you want her to do, Son? Sit home all day with the kids, cooking and cleaning, waiting for you to return home, so she can feed and fuck you to sleep like a good lil wife?"

"Well, damn, when you say it like that it sounds harsh." I frowned.

"That's 'cause it is harsh!" she yelled. "We don't marry to become less than, and that's exactly what happens when men like you aren't honest 'bout what you wanted from the very beginnin'. Y'all sweep us off our feet, then throw that same broom in our hands, expectin' us to be Molly the Maid during' the day and Suck It Susie at night, and sometimes that's not even enough. It's disrespectful."

My mom stared at me like she was ready to jump on my ass. I think everything she wanted to say to my father was being projected onto me.

"How is me wantin' Mecca to be at home wit' the kids, instead of hustlin' and bustlin' in the streets everyday, deliverin' mail, treatin' her like shit? We in Jersey, where we get all four seasons. Mecca be out there in all the elements, workin' hard, when she don't have to. And I help wit' the chores in our house and do my part when it comes to our girls, so you can't reduce me to what other men do, especially the man you chose to marry. His ass neva did a damn thing but boss all of us around." I kissed my teeth.

"See, that's what I'm talking 'bout right there." My mom laughed. It wasn't a regular giggle. That shit was more like a "fuck you" type of laugh. "Yo ass don't get a pat on the back or a praise dance for doin' what you supposed to do, Son. By the time yo monkey ass gets home, Mecca has done it all by herself. You just helpin' out with what's left to be done. You need to go to counselin', like yo brother did, so you can learn how to be a better husband to the woman you chose to marry."

"You knew 'bout that?" I quizzed, blowing my breath. "He just told me today. I'm always the last one to find shit out."

"It was my suggestion." She grinned. "The same way you came to me today, complaining, so did he."

"If that's yo suggestion for us, why didn't you go to counselin' to save yo marriage?"

When her eyes turned to slits, I knew I had fucked up.

"Who said I didn't, smart ass? You have no idea what I suffered through, or the hoops I jumped through, to keep our family together. Packing y'all up and walking away from the man I loved more than myself at that time wasn't as easy as it appeared. Failure was never an option for me. I stayed as long as I did, hoping he would change, but you can't make people be something they're not. Yo father wanted the image of a family but not the responsibility of it."

My mom sat back and crossed her legs.

"Well, I want the responsibility of mine, and we don't need no damn stranger tellin' us how to run our house or what's best for us. I thought maybe you could be the one to help us out but as usual, you will always make me out to be the bad guy. " She laughed.

"No, yo ass wants me to take yo side 'cause you my child, but it doesn't work like that with me. Wrong is wrong, but do what you want, Son. You came to me, so I'm doing my part as yo mother and only trying to guide you in the right direction. I want better for you and yo brother. I'm on the outside looking in and can see what y'all can't. But since you know it all, get cho yo ass up outta here and go home. You probably didn't even tell Mecca you were gonna be late." I stood to leave.

"A'ight, Ma, whateva. I'll holla at you lata, love you."

"Love you too, always, even when you get on my last muthafuckin' nerve. I'm yo momma first and yo friend second. Remember that."

She stood up and popped me on the side of my head. I deserved that because I was definitely set in my ways.

Once I got in my truck I sent Mecca a text, letting her know I stopped by my mom's house. When she responded back with the middle finger emoji, I ran my hands down my face and sighed. She probably was overwhelmed with the kids, and my little detour just made the situation worse.

Since I was already in the doghouse, I decided to stop at Strollo's Lighthouse and pick up some ice cream for dessert.

Once I made it home, Mecca looked like she had just reached her breaking point.

"Maya just bit Meelah on the arm, which is why she's cryin' like a banshee. Meesa decided to pee on the carpet instead of the potty while her sistas were fightin'. All three of 'em jumped some lil girl at the daycare today when she pushed Meesa down on the playground. They're suspended for two days, so hopefully yo mom can keep an eye on 'em for us. I was attacked by seagulls as I tried to eat my lunch on a bench at the beach this afternoon, so I just need five minutes to myself right now, please." Mecca's eyes were filled with tears.

"Sure, take as long as you need. I got 'em." I felt like shit.

"Don't let the sauce burn. It's almost done," she informed me before disappearing down the hall.

While Mecca took some time for herself, I made Maya apologize to her sister. She left her damn teeth print on Meelah's arm, so I cleaned it with some peroxide and put a Band-Aid on it. I made all three of them sit in a circle and hold hands while I cleaned up the pissy carpet and finished up dinner.

Everything that happened today was exactly why I wanted Mecca to be home. It wasn't about controlling her, but giving her some peace.

"I see you got things under control."

Mecca finally came out of hiding thirty minutes later. She looked refreshed and smelled amazing.

"Yeah, and you look like you just had a mini spa treatment."

My wife was the most beautiful woman I ever laid eyes on.

"Somethin' like that. I decided to take my shower now and wash the day away. It's been a rough one," she admitted.

"Well, I got yo favorite ice cream for lata, so I hope that helps," I informed her.

"Daddy, can we stop holdin' hands now," Maya asked.

She was the oldest, and the leader of the pack. I'm sure she threw the first punch during the fight at the daycare.

"Yeah, come sit down and stop givin' yo mom a hard time when I'm not here. You supposed to be helpin' her," I scolded.

All three girls got up and came to sit at the table. We had booster seats on their chairs to help them sit up correctly.

"What did you and yo mom talk 'bout?" Mecca quizzed while helping me bring the food to the table that I already set.

"Us, to be honest. I just wanted her opinion after talkin' to Savior today."

"So, you just goin' 'round talkin' 'bout me to yo family?" Mecca kissed her teeth.

"I talked to *our* family 'cause that's what they consider you, and yeah. My mom likes you more than me, shit."

She laughed, knowing it was true.

"Hopefully they set yo ass straight." Mecca cut her eyes at me.

"They both suggested therapy, which is crazy. Did you know yo sista and Savior were on the verge of divorcin' at some point?" Mecca's eyes got big as hell.

"No, I didn't! I'm callin' that bitch right now."

I stopped Mecca before she could get to her phone.

"Don't do that. Let's invite 'em ova for dinner and let her

explain why she didn't want us to know," I reasoned. "And I'm sure Savior didn't tell her he told me, so that's gone be a problem right there. He only said somethin' today tryin' to help me. If that nigga could take it back he would. They actually ended up in therapy, so they straight now."

"Okay, Imma let it go for now," Mecca agreed, reluctantly. Something told me she wasn't being honest. I know my wife, and she didn't do well with people keeping secrets from her. "And what problem do you have that Savior tried to fix?"

When Mecca folded her arms into her chest and rolled her neck, I knew it was about to be a long night.

Chapter Three

SIENNA HOLLAND

"Yes, babe, eat that pussy like it's a twice baked potato wit' sour cream and chives on it," I cooed.

Savior knew how to make my pussy wetter than the deep, blue sea. When his tongue flickered back and forth over my clit, my toes curled up. My body started to get hot, and the muscles in my stomach tightened. This man slurped and sucked until I creamed all over his face.

I had to muffle the sounds coming from out of my mouth with a pillow, so the kids couldn't hear me. My body convulsed like I was a fish out of water as Savior licked up every drop.

"Turn ova, so I can bust yo ass from behind," he demanded.

My husband was so cocky, and it turned me on. Without hesitating, I got down on all fours, putting my head down and ass up. I spread my legs far apart, giving him full access. When

Savior slid his big ass dick into my tight pussy, I clenched the sheets.

I had been fucking this man for ten years straight and still needed to adjust to his size. My walls stayed intact and welcomed the beating he gave them.

"Ooooooo, shit." I bit down on my lip.

"This pussy feel so fuckin' good. Damn, Sienna."

Hearing him compliment my womanly center heightened the pleasure I was already feeling, making me relax even more as my juices provided the lubrication for the penetration.

Ring! Ring!

The sound of my phone going off distracted me. When I looked over toward the nightstand, I saw it was Mecca calling me. She never called this late unless it was an emergency.

I reached over and answered my phone, putting it on speaker.

"Why the fuck didn't you tell me you went to marriage counselin', ho?" she quizzed.

Her voice was loud and laced with venom. I never told anyone about us going to counseling, not even my parents. Savior must have run his mouth to his brother, which was surprising.

He wasn't the gossiping, pillow talking type of man, and neither was Major to my knowledge. Whatever the case, Mecca was highly upset with me.

"Ahhhhhh, shit. Whew, lawd Jesus. Umm, I can't talk right now. I only answered 'cause I thought it was an emergency," I replied back with labored breathing.

Savior lifted up my ass cheeks and went in deeper. It felt like he was trying to see if he could touch my belly button from the inside.

"Yo marriage almost goin' to hell in a handbasket is an emergency..." Her words trailed off, and she got quiet.

"Ughhhhhhh, goddamn, babe," I moaned, not giving a damn about Mecca being able to hear us.

"Are y'all fuckin'?" Mecca quizzed. "All I keep hearin' is clappin' noises, and you soundin' like that nigga tryna snatch yo soul."

Savior kept putting in that work like I wasn't on the phone. This man wasn't slowing down at all. He proceeded to lay the pipe, thrusting in and out of me. The sound of his pelvic area crashing into my ass cheeks was the clapping sounds Mecca heard.

"Yes, we are, bitch!" I yelled.

"Then why would you answer, wit' cho nasty ass. Both of y'all get on my muthafuckin' nerves 'cause he coulda at least took a pause 'til I—"

I hung up on Mecca and started tossing my ass back at Savior. Though I was pissed that he shared our personal business, now wasn't the time to address it. He heard the entire conversation and knew I would be on his ass the minute we finished. Until then, I was going to let him continue fucking me like I was the town slut.

"Yeah, throw that shit." Savior encouraged my whorish behavior, so I decided to go all in.

I pushed myself up on my elbows to have better control

while I gripped the top of the mattress. My titties jiggled as I picked up my speed and let my tongue hang out my mouth like a panting dog.

"You 'bout to make me cum, Sienna, if you keep doin' that shit."

His words fell on deaf ears as I threw that thing in a circle. I was about to cum right with him, so there was no way I was about to show his ass any mercy.

"Fuck me harder!"

I placed my hand in between my legs and feverishly rubbed on the man in the little boat while Savior power drilled his dick into my swollen pussy. The intensity of the orgasm I experienced forced me to collapse onto the bed.

Savior never missed a beat and continued until he released while laying on my back. When he rolled over and tried to catch his breath, I sat up on my side and slapped him on his chest, hard as hell.

"Ouch! What the fuck was that for?" he quizzed, rubbing the spot I just smacked. "You busted before me this time."

"That's for tellin' Major 'bout the counselin' and whateva else the fuck you said to him. And don't lie and say you didn't."

I pulled the covers over me and turned my back to him, pissed that I now had to hear Mecca's mouth about why I didn't tell her myself.

"Yeah, get y'all raggedy asses up in here 'cause you got some explainin' to do."

Mecca greeted us at the door. She called me back the next day, at a decent hour this time, and invited us over for dinner. We had no plans for the weekend and accepted.

After Savior and I entered their house with our twin sons, who were seven years old, Mecca and I embraced in a hug. Even though she was upset with me, one thing we always did was show each other love.

Our relationship as sisters was intimate, and usually we told each other everything. She was my best friend, and the bond we shared from birth had always been a close one. We did everything together, including marrying brothers, and always had each other's back.

So, I understood why Mecca felt the way she did. I just hoped that once I explained my reasons for wanting to keep it to myself, she would forgive me.

"I know, I know, I know, damn. Let me get a drink in my hand before you jump on my ass." I waved my hand at her.

"Hey, auntie." The boys spoke in unison as they hugged Mecca.

"Hey, nephews, I missed you guys. Uncle Major is settin' up the game for y'all in the playroom. Go jump on his back."

Even though they had girls, Mecca and Major made sure they had stuff for the boys to do when they came over. They treated my sons as if they were their own and vice versa.

The boys ran off and Savior followed behind them, after giving Mecca a hug and slapping me on the ass.

"Where my bad ass nieces? I'm still laughin' at 'em whippin ass on the playground. At least you know they will stick together." I laughed.

"That's for damn sure," Mecca agreed, walking into the kitchen. "They're in their room. I'm sure they heard the boys, so their lil asses will come lookin' for you soon."

Just as Mecca finished talking, all I heard was three tiny voices calling my name.

"Auntie Enna!"

They ran up and hugged my legs, fighting for position.

"My babies." I gave them each a kiss on the cheek.

As fast as they came, they left.

"You know they love their cousins and don't have time for no one else when they 'round.

I just put the ziti in the oven, so we can make some drinks and go sit in the living room."

"Have you talked to mom?" I questioned as I washed my hands and grabbed a lemon to slice for garnish.

"No, why?" Mecca looked over at me with a raised eyebrow.

Our mom wasn't the most loving person in the world. She was short and abrupt with her words the majority of the time. My dad matched her energy, which was probably why they had been together for thirty-five years. They were made for each other.

"You didn't get the text she sent, askin' us to come over for a BBQ 'cause they haven't seen the kids yet this summer?"

"Yup, and I ignored it. The last time I took the girls to see her, all she did was put me down as a mother. She sounded like

Major, questionin' why I went back to work and didn't wait 'til all the kids were in elementary school. Yo mother even suggested boardin' school, then went on to say I was too clingy wit' 'em. So, disrespectfully, fuck her."

I understood where Mecca was coming from. The relationship we had with our mom was strained from the beginning. She never hugged us or said the words "I love you". If we said it to her, she would just smile. Our father was no better.

In my mind, they only had us to say they had kids. Both our parents were successful doctors who had their own medical practice together. With their busy lives, they had no business even having children because we were not their priority.

We spent more time at our grandmothers' houses than our own. They showered us with love and affection and basically raised us. If it wasn't for them, I don't know how Mecca and I would have turned out.

"If you not goin', I damn sure ain't goin'. Savior can't stand 'em and would rather sit his ignorant ass in the car wit' the windows rolled up, with no AC, before he steps foot in their house." We laughed. "Daddy had the nerve to tell him his name sounded stupid, and the only savior he recognized was Jesus Christ, so he would call him Jonathan instead."

"Jonathan?" Mecca shook her head as she poured the liquor over the ice in our glasses.

"Girl, bye. Now, you know the guy they wanted me to marry was named Jonathan. Their neighbor Ms. Mary's son," I reminded her, adding some cranberry and orange juice to the glasses.

I put the lemon slices on top, grabbed both glasses, then made my way to the living room while Mecca carried in the charcuterie board she had already prepared.

"That's right. I almost forgot 'bout him. They don't like Major's name either. Daddy calls him minor when referring to him. In person, he doesn't call Major anything, just nods his head at him."

We got comfortable on the sofa, just as the guys were walking in.

"Y'all ain't make us nothin' to drink?" Major quizzed.

"I put some beers in the freezer for y'all. Get 'em out before they freeze," Mecca replied.

Once they had their beverages, the guys each took a seat on the couch next to us. It was huge and could easily fit six adults comfortably.

Mecca and I snuggled up on this couch with the kids plenty of days and watched movies together during the winter months. Our kids will know what it felt like to grow up in a tight knit family full of love.

"Okay, so let's just dive right on in." Mecca smacked her lips. "When did you guys go to counselin', and why did y'all try to play in our face and not tell us what was goin' on?"

My sister took a sip of her drink and looked directly into my eyes. I hated when she did that because it felt like she could read my mind and feel my soul. That twin connection was real.

Chapter Four

MECCA

I searched Sienna's eyes for the truth. Her ass knew she had no choice but to come clean.

"Last summer and to be honest, we had no plans of tellin' anyone. Ms. Peggy only knew 'cause it was her suggestion to Savior. It's embarrassin' when you have to seek outside help for some shit you signed up for. We said for better or for worse and when the worse came, our asses almost crashed and burned." Sienna's eyes filled with tears.

"When I asked if you and Savoir were good last year in the Bahamas, you looked me in the face and said yes. I knew somethin' was off, but you neva lied to me before, so I had no reason to not believe you." I shook my head.

We always took a family trip every year to an island with our husbands and the kids. Last year we went to the Bahamas. This year we were going to Bali in the winter. No matter where we chose, we always stayed for two weeks to give ourselves enough time to enjoy everything the island had to offer.

"At that time we were good, so I thought. When we got back from the trip, Savior seemed different. He walked around wit' an attitude for 'bout a week before I said anythin' to him. I figured it had somethin' to do with work, so imagine my surprise when this nigga said I was the problem."

Sienna wiped the tears from her face that finally made their way to the surface.

"I didn't say you were the problem," Savior corrected. "You came to that conclusion on yo own. All I said was we needed to figure out how to probably communicate wit' each other 'cause—"

"You said I talked to you like you were a child." Sienna cut him off.

"See, you won't even let me finish my sentence." Savior took a swig from his bottle and shook his head.

From the way they were acting, Savior and Sienna might end up back in therapy.

"And I apologize." Sienna cut her eyes. "Just make sure you tell it right."

"As I was saying, *we* needed to learn how to talk to each other wit' respect. The entire trip, when we weren't 'round y'all, she talked to me crazy and made what was supposed to be a relaxin' vacation a miserable one for me. My response coulda been better 'cause I matched her energy, but Sienna has a way of makin' you feel this small when she talks to you." Savior held his thumb and pointer finger about a quarter inch apart from each other as a visual aid.

“Now, that part is true,” I agreed, and Sienna shot me a dirty look.

Her mouth was definitely a lethal weapon when she got going. By the time Sienna got done telling you how she felt, you were ready to beat her face in. It was what she said and how she said it.

“Thank you, Mecca. She used to talk to me like I was one of the damn kids,” Savior complained.

“That’s ’cause you act like one sometimes. Our boys always listen to me when I speak to ’em. I have to say somethin’ to you multiple times.”

“They be scared, that’s why.” Savior laughed, and Sienna playfully mushed him on the side of his head.

“Whateva,” she sneered.

“I still feel a way that you didn’t think you could confide in me.” Major rubbed my back when he saw me getting emotional.

“If I told you what was goin’ on, you woulda automatically took my side. I didn't need any outside influences if I wanted to save my marriage. Savior and I needed to work it out among ourselves. It was my idea, not his, to keep it a secret. I wanted everyone to still believe that we had the perfect marriage when in reality, there isn’t one. And truth be told, during our sessions I realized I actually was the problem,” Sienna admitted.

“Shit, if counselin’ got Sienna admittin’ fault, we definitely need to go.” Major laughed.

I turned my neck so fast in his direction, you could feel the gust of wind that was created.

“What’s that supposed to mean?” I could feel my nostrils flaring.

“Maybe you too can see the errors of yo ways,” he answered, with a grin on his face.

I downed my drink and sat the glass on the coffee table in front of me.

“Whew, lawd, no he didn’t.”

Sienna leaned back and sunk down into the couch while Savior dropped his head.

“What’s my problem, Sir?”

I interlock my fingers as I let my elbows rest on my knees. Major knew when I called him Sir, it was on.

“For starters, you keep lettin’ the kids sleep in our bed, cock blockin’. We barely get any alone time to do adult things anymore. And you already know how I feel ’bout you workin’. You almost had a whole meltdown the other day when yo day got a lil crazy. Whenever I try to let you know how I feel, you cut me off or walk away. I feel unheard and neglected.”

My first thought was to call Major a bitch ass nigga, but I held my tongue. We promised to never hit below the belt, so I had to choose my words wisely.

“How dare you bring up the moment I had the other day. You ain't shit for that, and it was your idea to have the kids back-to-back, thinkin’ I would stay home. But when I went back to work, your plan fell apart. Now, we have to share our bed wit’ the kids you wanted and you mad? Maybe we do need to go to counselin', so you can see the errors of your ways." I looked over at Sienna. "Can you please text me the number of the person you guys saw."

"Umm, yeah, she's really good and doesn't choose sides. We still see her every three months, virtually. She encouraged me to journal, which helps a lot and allows me to free my mind. Maybe you should try it before you go."

"It may not seem like it today, but we came a long way. Each week we take one day for ourselves. My mom keeps the boys. She probably will do the same for y'all too," Savior added.

"Shit, no she won't. Mommy watched 'em while they were suspended, and said they can't come over any more without us. It was the first time she had all three of 'em together by herself. She had our girls sittin' on the steps outside wit' all their shit when Mecca pulled up to get 'em each day." They laughed.

"I'm 'bout to get the food outta the oven. Y'all can help the kids wash their hands while Sienna and I set the table." Major tried to rub my butt when I stood up.

I swatted his hand away and cut my eyes at him. If he thought he had blue balls now, they were about to be black by the time he got some of this good pussy again. He could have the bed all to himself because I planned on camping out in the girl's room until we went to therapy.

"Hello, I'm Wanda Stevenson. It's a pleasure to meet you both. Please have a seat."

The counselor greeted us when we walked into her office and pointed to a couch for us to sit on. We managed to get an appointment two weeks from the day Sienna gave me her contact information.

Major was able to move around his schedule to take the same lunch break as me. We had no choice but to come when the kids were at daycare. It was our intake session, so it would only be for thirty minutes, instead of the normal hour.

I made sure to google our counselor and found her ass on Facebook too. She appeared to be single and very lowkey. The only pictures she shared were ones of her cats and plants. Sienna said I was being extra, but I needed to know who I was about to tell all my business too.

This heifer had the nerve to only accept cash or card as payment, which aggravated me. Hopefully our insurance will reimburse us because she charged $125 an hour. If she didn't come highly recommended by the yelp reviews, I would have chosen someone else. Even though my sister said she was good, I needed to make sure others felt the same way about Miss Stevenson.

"Hello, I'm Mrs. Holland, and this is my husband Mr. Holland. Thank you for squeezin' us into yo schedule," I replied as we sat down next to each other.

Miss Steven sat across from us in a plush, cream colored chair. She had her hair pulled up into a bun and was dressed like an old ass lady. The clothes she wore were oversized, and her glasses sat right on the edge of her nose. I had to stop myself from pushing them up on her face.

Even though she appeared to look like a librarian who needed a makeover, you could still see the undeniable beauty she possessed underneath it all.

"Since this is our initial meeting, I just want to get to know who you are and what brought you guys here today. How about we start with you, Mr. Holland."

Miss Stevenson crossed her legs and smiled like she was doing a Colgate commercial.

"You can call me Major, and I'm just a man who loves his family. We here 'cause my wife and I aren't on the same page when it comes to how our household should run."

"Bruh, really. We are here 'cause he thinks I'm some weak ass woman who can't take care of our home while workin' outside of it. Major knew when we decided to make a life together exactly who I was. Once the ring went on and the kids started comin', he switched up." I frowned. "And he complains 'bout our sex life, which I think is the root of all our issues."

"I can see by your facial expression, Mrs. Holland, you are very upset." She looked over at me.

"You can call me Mecca," I replied sarcastically. Even though I introduced us as Mr. and Mrs. Holland, Major wanted to be on a first name basis, so I matched his energy. "And I'm beyond pissed. My husband is tryin' to play in my face, and I don't like it."

"Can you elaborate further for me, so that I have a clear understanding of what you mean?"

"Major told me how his father basically forced his mom into bein' a housewife. My husband said when he got married, his wife would never be treated that way, but he lied. This man now wants me to quit my job and stay home, so I can cook, clean, and watch the kids all day. I love him, but he got me fucked up." I shrugged my shoulders.

"What was the reason you changed your mind, Major? It seems as if you told her everything she needed to hear then once the ink dried on the paper, you decided to go off script." Major blew his breath.

I got excited when she questioned him and allowed a slight grin to form on my face. Finally, someone else, besides me and his mother, was checking his ass.

"She got it all wrong. I want her to be home in order to have time for herself and us. The kids can still go to daycare a few days a week, so I'm not tryna make her be a slave as she tries to describe it. I make enough money to cover all our bills and everything else. The majority of the money she makes does go into the shared expense account for the house, but that's her choice. We can survive without it," he explained.

"That's true, but the point yo ass keep missin' is that I want to help. I like makin' my own money and helpin' to pay the bills in *our* house. My name is on the paperwork as well. Our daughters will see that their mommy works just as hard as their daddy. Even though my mom is bat shit crazy, the one thing she taught me was to always have yo own.

"And more than anything else, I like the seein' all the people on my route everyday. They have become part of my life and look for me. Major never takes the time to ask me 'bout my job or how it makes me feel. He just sees me as the mail lady who works too hard for nothing. I love what I do."

I swallowed the lump that formed in my throat as I fought back my tears.

"Well, I see we have a lot to unpack here. I went over the paperwork you filled out online and even though you two have been together for ten years, your children are very young and close in age. That adds to the stress of everything else, and usually that falls on the mom. I'm sure that's why your sex life changed." Major hung his head.

"He doesn't see it that way and expects me to sexually perform all night, every night, like I used to before we had our girls, but that's a discussion for another day."

"Shit, I'm just askin' for a performance. The kids in our bed every night is a problem," Major complained.

"Wait, the kids are still sleeping in your bed?" Miss Stevenson pushed her glasses up on her face and stared at me.

"Yes," I replied as her eyes burned a hole in me.

"That's a huge problem, and one we need to resolve immediately." When she said that, Major smiled so hard I wanted to punch all his teeth out. "Tonight, I want you to put those kids back in their bed if they try to come and take over yours. It's okay for them to sleep with you here and there, but not every night."

"That's all I'm sayin'." Major put up his hands like he was surrendering.

"I also have a class I teach on the side that would be great for you guys. We can discuss that once we make some progress with the issues at hand. And Major, don't get too excited because I agreed with you about the kids. You are dead wrong when it comes wanting your wife to stop working. We need to find a healthy balance in all areas, and I promise to help you to do just that." I laughed because she took the wind right out of his sails.

Major stood to leave then reached his hand out to help me up. My husband has always been a gentleman, even when he was aggravated with me.

"Thank you, babe." I kissed his lips.

"Yeah, whateva." He squeezed my butt.

"See, that's what we want, black love. Most people leave here ready to fight on the first day. The fact that you guys were affectionate toward each other says a lot. Check your email when you get home. I'm going to send you some exercises to do for our next session. See you soon."

As we left the office, Major and I walked hand-in-hand back to the car. I was hesitant at first and didn't know what to expect but now, coming here was the best decision we could have made. Miss Stevenson was everything Sienna said she was, and I looked forward to our next session.

Chapter Five

WANDA "STRAWBERRY" STEVENSON

After the Hollands left my office, I immediately hopped onto my computer and pulled up the information on another couple with that same last name, who I helped in the past and still kept in touch with.

Due to patient confidentiality, I couldn't ask Major and Mecca if they were related to Sienna and Savior. When I received their online form I recognized the name right away, but sometimes people share the same last name but aren't related. It wasn't until I stared into Mecca's face, which was the same as Sienna's, that I knew they had to be twins.

Sienna mentioned having a sister who was married to her husband's brother, talk about keeping it in the family, but left the twin part out. These brothers married bookends, but they were nothing alike, especially in the way they carried themselves and spoke.

From what I gathered, Mecca wasn't about to allow Major to force her hand. She seemed like the type of woman who spoke up for herself and wasn't going to let anyone make her do anything she didn't want to. On the other hand, Sienna put on this tough girl act, but inside wasn't as strong as she appeared.

She cried a lot during our sessions, and it pissed me off. I hated a weak woman who couldn't control her emotions. Savior used it to his advantage and convinced Sienna it was all her fault. As their counselor I should have helped Sienna find her voice, but I didn't. Instead, I agreed with him.

Sienna didn't deserve my help because she lacked a certain strength that was definitely present in her sister. Unlike Sienna, Mecca wouldn't allow herself to be placed inside of a box.

She reminded me of the type of wife I would be the day I settled down. At the age of forty the sand in my hourglass was running out, but my man was in a compromising situation, so my personal life was at a standstill.

I also don't think Major really wanted Mecca to be a housewife. He wanted her to make time for him. If I could help them balance work and family life, they would be just fine. It was couples like them that got my juices flowing.

When they fought, they fought hard. The only problem was they didn't know how to make up with the same passion they argued with. If they did, I guarantee you they wouldn't have made it into my office. The fact that lack of sex was a huge issue for them told me the only thing being twisted and folded up in their house was the laundry.

In my line of business, I found that the couples who learned how to have soul-snatching, mind blowing sex after a big blow up rarely needed my help for long, which was why I started my master class called Breathless.

I gave private lessons to couples who struggled to find their way sexually. In just three weeks, I taught them how to leave each other breathless. Whether they had five minutes or five hours, all my couples learned how to use that time to make their partner beg for mercy.

Hopefully, Major and Mecca would take me up on my offer once we got them back to the way they were before they had kids. I didn't invite Sienna and Savior because my course was only for couples I liked. If I couldn't vibe with your energy, then Breathless wasn't for you.

Just thinking about the next class I was going to teach later on tonight made my pussy moist. I got up and locked my door. There was no one else for the rest of the day, so I could satisfy myself without any interruptions.

After drawing the shades and lighting a candle to set the mood, I pulled out the purple bag my friend Delilah put together for me last Valentine's Day from my desk drawer and made my way over to the couch Major and Mecca were just sitting on. Stripping down to nothing, I sat down and unzipped the bag.

I removed the bottle of hot and spicy, edible lube and squeezed some on my fingers. Spreading my legs apart, I slid my fingers between the slit in my pussy and rubbed it all over my clit. When it began to warm up, I removed the pink and gold bullet vibrator from the bag. This thing was small but packed a powerful punch. It had ten settings, and I planned on enjoying each one.

I relaxed back on the couch, lengthwise, and threw my right leg over the back of it while letting the other one hang off the edge with my foot on the floor. Putting the vibrator on the first setting felt like a little tease as I glided it back forth over my throbbing clit. Number two wasn't much better, so I moved on to three. The vibration picked up some, but it still felt like I was using my fingers.

When I pushed it up to four, I closed my eyes and massaged my titties with my free hand. My juices started to flow, so it was only right to go to the next setting. I was halfway there now and knew my climax was on the horizon once my clit began to swell.

As my thumb pressed the button to make it go to number six, the humming sound coming from the vibrator got louder. I moved that thang up, down, and around the little man in the boat, about to make his ass tip over.

At seven, a tingling sensation radiated throughout my body. My nipples were harder than two pebbles and sweat formed on my brow.

"Ahhhhh," I moaned out loud, feeling all the pleasure from the tool that was also making my fingers numb at this point.

My breathing started to become labored at setting eight as I grinded my hips into the cushion. Giving my clit a slight break in action, I moved the vibrator to the opening of my womanly center.

"Ssssss, fuck!" I yelled out.

If someone was passing by my office they probably thought I was in here getting done dirty, but this was a one woman show.

Pressing the button once again, I was now at nine and ready to cream all over my fingers. Trying to hold my hand still as the sensation consumed me wasn't an easy task. I had moved the vibrator back to my clit and had it positioned on the exact spot that was making my nipples even harder. My pelvic muscles tightened, and my body convulsed.

During my climax, I put the vibrator on its final setting. My now fully numbed fingertips held it in place while my sweet nectar dripped out of my wet and sticky pussy. I could feel the juices down the crack of my ass.

Turning the vibrator off, I laid there and enjoyed the little spasms that still rippled throughout my body. I made a mental note to have the couch cleaned before my next session.

"How have you guys been? Are you still practicing healthy boundaries and making time for each other?"

I was having a virtual session with Sienna and Savior Holland. Usually we had it in the evening, but my earlier appointments ran late, so I had to push it back to eight o'clock. They agreed because we wouldn't be on for long. My three month check-in only lasted for fifteen minutes. It gave me enough time to find out how they were doing and offer any advice if needed. Actually, it was unnecessary in my opinion.

Most couples could figure it out on their own once they were given the proper tools but some, like these two here, still wanted to hang onto the umbilical cord. They were needy and got on my damn nerves. Not Savior so much, but Sienna's whining ass made my skin crawl.

"We've been doin' good. Savior did suggest I find a part time job to give me somethin' to do while the kids are in school, so I'm thinkin' of actually volunteerin' at our local ASPCA instead. I love animals and hopefully can find a dog for our family to adopt while I'm there."

This was the dumb shit I was talking about. Savior suggested she earn a few dollars, but Sienna took it upon herself to give her time away instead. There was nothing wrong with volunteering, but one of the issues they had was about her spending money like she earned it.

Savior mentioned he liked the idea of Sienna being home when the kids were young, but thought she would go back to work once they were in school. He didn't complain about her choosing to stay home, since he made enough to support their home, until she developed an online shopping habit.

"Don't you have a degree in marketing? I'm confused as to why you wouldn't want to put it to use. You can even work from home these days," I suggested.

"That's what I said." Savior chimed in. "I told her to contact her old job, and see if they have any openings. She left on good terms, so they should take her back. I would have her work for my company, but it would be a conflict of interest. They have a nepotism clause in my contract."

Savior was in upper management for a chain of grocery stores. He put in a lot of hours, which was one of Sienna's complaints. She had a lot of nerve to whine about her man working hard for them when she got to sit home all day, doing absolutely nothing.

"Whether I work at home or in an office, if the school calls I have to stop what I'm doin' and deal wit' it. If the kids are sick and have to stay home, it's my problem. He damn sure not gonna help," Sienna fired back. "I cook, clean, and do laundry. Basically, I'm the fuckin' maid for the kids and this nigga."

Savior's eyes widened when Sienna pointed her finger toward him and frowned her face.

"It seems to me that you guys might need to come back in for a full session. Obviously there is still some tension and unresolved issues." I looked at them both.

"We were fine until yo ass brought up my degree. He didn't have an issue when I mentioned it the other day. Now that he has an audience of one, it's a problem. Imma 'bout to get off of this. I'm startin' to think you don't like me anyway," Sienna spewed.

I wanted to say I don't, but that would be unprofessional of me. Instead, I took a deep breath before responding.

"First of all, I'm not here to choose sides. I'm sorry that you feel I don't like you. I have never gave you any reason to feel th—"

"Kiss my ass, Miss Stevenson. All I did was praise you to everyone I knew 'cause you did help us, even though I always felt a way. I thought I was buggin', so I kept my feelings to myself, but tonight proved I was right. You always have a scowl on yo face when it's my turn to talk. Savior does no wrong in yo eyes. Just admit you don't like me and push those ugly ass glasses up on yo face. You look stupid as hell. I know you feel 'em always slidin' down on yo nose."

Sienna hopped up and walked away, leaving Savior alone and me completely stunned.

"Umm, I don't know what to say. I'm sure my wife didn't mean anythin' she just said."

"Yes the fuck I did, and you got five seconds to leave that zoom before I cut the power off," Sienna threatened.

I could no longer see her, but she made sure her presence was known.

"Listen, I'm here if you guys need me. Even if she doesn't want to participate, I can help you communicate with her. Just—"

My words were cut off when their screen went black. At that moment I wished I was a fly on their wall.

Chapter Six

SAVIOR HOLLAND

"What the fuck you do that for? You probably scared the damn kids," I yelled.

Sienna's crazy ass actually went to the breaker box and cut off the power.

"Oh, please, I only cut off the power in here and the kitchen, then turned it right back on. The boys are fine."

We were sitting in the living room on the first floor. The breaker box was located in the kitchen, so she was able to access it quickly.

"You were rude as hell to Miss Stevenson. I hope you apologize to her tomorrow once you pull yo head out cho ass. And stop orderin' me around like I'm yo third son. We already addressed this. If I did that to you, you would be on the phone right now, cryin' to yo sista."

I was sick of Sienna's bullshit. She was just mad because everything Miss Stevenson said was true. Sienna had a problem with anyone who didn't agree with her.

"It's called couples therapy. If I walk away, there is no couple, so yo ass shoulda automatically left too. You wanna continue to sit there and smile all up in her raggedy ass face. If you had a problem wit' me volunteerin' instead of workin', you shoulda said somethin' when I first mentioned it. You wait and try to embarrass me in front of her." Sienna's voice cracked.

She always resorted to tears to get her way. That was where Sienna and Mecca were different. Mecca didn't cry at the drop of a dime. She had a harder exterior than her twin. They were both naturally emotional creatures as women, but Sienna always turned on the waterworks every chance she got. Mecca would have to be pushed to her limits before she cried.

I watched her and Major go at it plenty of times, and she held her own. She actually broke his ass down. He said she was the tougher one out of the two of them, but I didn't believe him until I saw her in action. Sienna's bark was louder than her bite. Mecca would just bite.

"How did I embarrass you? Stop actin' like I didn't tell you to call yo old job. You just mad that she didn't agree wit' you goin' to babysit some cats and dogs." I laughed, pissing her off even more.

"Fuck you and her. You can sleep down here or in the guest room, since you have so much to say. Now, laugh at that, muthafucka."

Sienna gave me the finger and walked off. I went into the

kitchen and grabbed a cold beer from out of the fridge. Opening the cabinet, I snatched the bottle of vodka from the top shelf and poured myself up a shot.

I wasn't going to sleep on no damn couch when I paid all the bills. Sienna was out of her rabbit ass mind if she thought that shit. I had a remedy for her ass, though.

After downing the shot and drinking the beer, I climbed the steps to the second floor. The boys were already showered and in bed. They had camp tomorrow, so it was lights out for them right before we got online.

When I entered our bedroom, Sienna was sprawled out across the bed on her stomach, crying into the phone. I already knew she called her sister as soon as she got upstairs.

"Hang up the phone," I demanded, closing the door behind me.

"Go to hell." Sienna tried to get up, and I snatched the phone out of her hand.

"Bye, Mecca. She'll call you tomorrow. Have a good night." I ended the call then placed her phone on the table next to our bed.

Now on her feet, Sienna walked up on me. At six one, I towered over her petite but shapely frame. Being that I was six inches taller than her, she had to look up at me.

Her dark, brown eyes were intoxicating even when Sienna was upset. When she parted her thick, supple lips to speak, I silenced her with a kiss. She bit my bottom lip and tried to pull away from me, but I scooped her up in one swift move and slammed her onto our bed.

I pinned Sienna down with her hands above her head as I straddled her. She tried to squirm free but wasn't going anywhere.

"Listen, I didn't get married to sleep alone. I'm yo husband, and you will show me some damn respect. Don't you ever tell me to sleep somewhere else. You been doin' what the hell you wanted for the last ten years, and I allowed it 'cause there is nothin' in this world I wouldn't do for you, but that shit stops right now. Stop actin' like a spoiled ass brat who didn't get her way, and be the woman who stole my heart all those years ago. I'm here and ain't goin' nowhere... ever! I just need you to meet me in the middle. Do you understand me?"

Sienna's face, which was full of tension, began to soften. Her eyes filled with tears that began to trickle down the side of her face and drip into her ears.

"Yes, I understand," she mumbled.

I licked her lips, then softly kissed all over her face. Her beautiful, brown skin was flawless. She had a natural beauty that captivated me the moment I laid eyes on her.

When my lips made their way to her neck, Sienna let out a soft moan. I stood to my feet and snatched off the sweats she was wearing. Crawling back onto the bed, I buried my face between her legs and started eating Sienna's pussy through the sheer panties she had.

"Shit, Savior, goddamn," she cooed.

I pulled them off to give myself full access once she was warmed up. Diving back in, I sucked on her clit like I was trying to get the nectar from a honeysuckle. My tongue navigated its way up and down the length of her pussy, making Sienna squirm beneath me.

When she pushed her pussy into my face and grinded her hips, I started slurping that muthafucka up even faster.

"Ahhhhh! Sssssss, whew," Sienna moaned.

"Turn over," I demanded.

When Sienna rolled over and got on her knees, I ate her ass until she collapsed onto the bed from the orgasm that caused her body to become weak.

"Geesh," she let out.

"We just gettin' started. Get cho ass back up here."

I pulled Sienna up by the back of her shirt and took it off. As I kissed her shoulders, I unhooked the bra she still had on and freed her full, bouncy breast. My hands cupped them as she relaxed back against my chest.

After fondling her for a few minutes, I wrapped my hand around her hair and pushed my wife back down on all fours. Sienna's ass was in the perfect position for me to enter her from behind. I stood up and stripped out of my clothes, then climbed back on the bed. Sienna's pussy was still wet and welcomed me with a warm hug.

I placed my free hand on the small of her back and started thrusting in and out. As I pulled on her hair, it forced Sienna to form a deep arch in her back.

"Ooooo, Imma get it together. I promise not to speak to you again like that."

When Sienna started rambling, it excited me even more. I dug deeper, making my strokes long and hard by pulling all the way out, until the tip of my dick was at her opening, then sliding it back in with force. My pelvic area crashed into her ass over and over again.

"You say somethin'? I can't hear you." I grinned.

"Babe, you heard me." Sienna was moaning and breathing hard. "You 'bout to make me cum."

Once I heard those words, I released the grip I had on her hair, held onto her hips and fucked Sienna until she creamed all over me. I released seconds later, pulled out, and slapped her on the ass. Now that we had come to an understanding, we could both go to sleep satisfied and at peace.

"Dana, can you please print out the end of the month reports for all the stores in Ocean and Monmouth counties. I need them put in alphabetical order according to their city. Make sure you highlight the totalprofits for each one, then bring them to me. Thank you."

I spoke to my executive assistant in my work voice through the intercom on my phone.

"Yes, Mr. Holland. I will get on that right away," Dana replied.

Even though she was cool as hell, I always kept it professional with my staff. There weren't too many of us in upper management at first, therefore we had to set the tone in regards to how they viewed us.

When I was given the opportunity to hire my own team, I

made sure they looked just like me on purpose. We all went out to dinner our first week working together, and I let them know I was running a tight ship and would only accept black excellence. They knew we already had to work twice as hard just to get where we were, and there was no room for failure.

There were eight stores under my management, and every month all eight of them out performed their surrounding competition, including the ones controlled by my colleagues. I've been in this position for three years and once my team and I started crushing the numbers, the management positions suddenly became more diverse.

Twenty minutes later, Dana entered my office with the work I requested in her hand. My office door was open, so she walked right in.

"Here you are, Mr. Holland. Is there anything else you need me to do for you before I head out to lunch, in about fifteen minutes?"

Dana stood in front of my desk, with her back to the door, wearing an emerald green, v-neck dress that hugged every curve on her body. She kept her hair in a chin length bob but would part it in different ways. Even though you could tell she wore makeup, it always looked natural.

If I wasn't a married man who only had eyes for my wife, I definitely would have been in a compromising situation with Dana. She had a husband, but he wasn't shit. The nights we had to work late, Dana would talk about him. They had two kids and had been together since they were in middle school, so she felt trapped.

I tried to tell her she deserved better, but it went in one ear and out the other. She was still young, only twenty-five, but had a good head on her shoulders. Hopefully, Dana realized her worth before it lost too much value dealing with a knucklehead who only diminished it.

She was actually the one who suggested Miss Stevenson to me after my mother told us to go to counseling. Dana said she researched a lot of counselors when she tried to get her husband to go, but he refused. According to her, Miss Stevenson was the best around, and I would have to agree. I'm sure Sienna would beg to differ.

"No, but you enjoy yourself. It's a beautiful day out," I answered.

"Can I bring you something back?" Dana inquired. "I'm going to the Mexican spot that has those tacos you like."

"That won't be necessary, sweetie. I have his lunch right here."

Dana spun around on her heels when she heard my wife's voice.

"Hello, Mrs. Holland. It's always a pleasure to see you. I'll leave you two alone."

Sienna sashayed her way over to me as Dana exited the office, closing the door behind her.

"Why did you have to call her sweetie like that? You know those are fightin' words to black women when said in the tone you used." I laughed.

"You know I don't care for her ass, but you keep on your

staff anyway. And if she ever tried me, I would beat the shit outta her."

Sienna cut her eyes at me and sat the picnic basket she was carrying down on my desk.

"Stop bein' mean and come give me a kiss. This is a nice surprise."

I had no idea my wife was stopping by today, and neither did Dana. Usually Sienna always told me ahead of time whenever she wanted to stop by. I would let Dana know as a heads up. She was very aware of how Sienna felt about her.

Dana has never done anything to Sienna to warrant such treatment from her, but Sienna thought otherwise. She said I needed to hire someone that was ugly and closer to retirement age to be my assistant. In her eyes, Dana was waiting for the right opportunity to make her move on me. The fact that we worked so closely together and had to pull late nights sometimes made Sienna feel a certain way. I tried telling her she was insecure and almost lost my life.

"Who's bein' mean?" Sienna questioned after giving me a peck on the lips. "She had no business tryin' to feed my man. Let her worry 'bout what her husband is eatin' for lunch. And her dress is inappropriate for the workplace."

"You used to dress like that when you worked, so it sounds like the pot callin' the kettle black." I kissed my teeth.

"Say somethin' else in defense to her, and Imma fire her ass myself." Sienna was serious.

"Chill, bruh. What's in the basket?" I quizzed.

"Well, I figured we could have an office picnic to celebrate my goin' back to work. They offered me a part-time position and will work with my schedule." Sienna smiled.

After I took back control and put it down on her ass, the next morning she contacted her old job. They told her to come in immediately for an interview.

"That's great news. I'm so proud of you, babe. Lock the door, so I can show you just how much." I licked my lips.

"You don't have to tell me twice."

Sienna sensually walked over to the door, stripping along the way. My dick instantly bricked up. By the time she made it back to me, Sienna only had on a thong and her bra. I unloosened my tie and took it off, then unbuttoned my shirt and tossed it to the side after removing it.

When my wife turned around, removed her undergarments, and bent over, I grabbed Sienna by the hips and sucked on her pussy like it was a frozen pineapple flavored Now and Later.

"Yes, my king, just like that. Ahhhhhh!" Sienna yelled out.

She was being extra loud on purpose, and I loved every minute of it. Thank goodness I had a corner office on the top floor. We were about to turn my office into a brothel.

Chapter Seven

MECCA

"No, you did not go to Savior's office and cut up like that." I stared at Sienna with wide eyes.

We met for lunch at the Windmill to catch up. They had tables with benches outside, so after getting our food we sat down to relax. It was a Saturday afternoon, and the guys were at my house watching the kids. It had been a minute since Sienna and I were able to go out with just us. As sisters it was important to keep our friendship at the forefront. With us both being mothers and wives, our individual families always came first.

"Girl, bye. We fucked all over his office, and I was in there actin' like we were in a private hotel room and not at his job. I wanted Dana to hear how my pussy made Savior moan my name," Sienna spewed.

"Listen, I get it. If Major had an assistant that looked like Dana, I would be a lil insecure too." Sienna gave me a nasty look.

"You sound just like him and 'bout to piss me off. My feelings for her have nothin' to do wit' bein' insecure and everythin' to do wit' the fact that she dresses like a slut. Yes, Dana is very attractive. There's no denying that, but tricks like her always go for the married ones." Sienna kissed her teeth.

"But she's married." I laughed. "Leave that girl alone. She's just doing her job and doesn't have to dress like an old maid. If she crosses the line, I'm sure Savior would put her in her place. He loves you and has never given you a reason not to trust him." I tried to reason with Sienna as I tore into my cheese fries.

The fact that I had on jean shorts and a t-shirt while she was dressed for a cocktail party to come eat a burger said it all. Sienna wore tight ass clothes and always looked like she was about to do a photoshoot, so why Dana dressing the same way bothered her was beyond me. Now that I think about it, Sienna might not be wrong in her thought process. If Savior loved that about her, he might also secretly desire the same thing about Dana, which was why he hired her in the first place.

Hmmmm, he definitely had a type.

When Savior and Major first met us, Savior noticed us first and went straight for Sienna, even though we were dressed the same. My sister just decided to take her shirt and tie a back knot in it to show off her belly button ring. She also got her jeans a size smaller, so it could hug her ass tighter.

"Yeah, I guess. Let's switch subjects before I go all the way down the rabbit hole. How's counseling goin'?" Sienna inquired.

"Really good, surprisingly. I was against it at first, but Miss Stevenson has really been helpin' us out. Of course Major and I had to do the work, but her advice has been spot on. The girls have been sleepin' in their own bed, so our sex life has gotten a lil better. It's just that wit' the kids and work, some days I don't enjoy it like I used to. But Major can't get enough of this good, good, so I lay there and go through the motions in order to please him," I admitted.

"You better get it together and pop that pussy right for him before someone else does. These bitches out here waitin' for the opportunity to take our places. Don't make it easy for 'em, sis. Take the same advice you would give me." Sienna bit into her burger.

"Well, Miss Stevenson invited us to this private class called Breathless. It's for couples who are struggling sexually or those who just want to learn how to please their significant other better. We start next month. She wants to make sure Major and I keep makin' progress before allowin' us to participate. Hopefully that puts a spring in my step."

"See, I'm glad I cussed her ass out 'cause why didn't she offer the class to Savior and I." I raised my brow.

"Beats me," I shrugged my shoulders. "And you never told me you cussed her out 'cause Savior rudely ended our call, so he could gather yo ass right quick. You know he hates when you do that cryin' bullshit. Now, what happened?"

When Sienna explained everything that went on, I felt

conflicted. She was my sister, and we always stuck together, but Miss Stevenson had been such a great help to Major and I.

"I feel like we might need to fall back too. If she don't fuck wit' you, then she don't fuck wit' me," I explained.

"Nah, don't stop on my account. Savior said I was dead wrong and needed to apologize. I will, but when I get good and ready. Don't let my childish ways affect yo progress. Enjoy the class and let me know if her funny lookin' ass teaches you somethin' new. I'm sure Miss Stevenson is a certified freak." We both laughed.

"Yeah, she probably has a killa shape underneath all those clothes. Everythin' she wears is too big and just doesn't look right on her."

"Including them ugly ass glasses, fuckin' bitch. I hate her." Sienna sighed.

We talked some more and finished our food before heading back to the house. The guys had been left alone with the kids long enough. Hopefully, no one needed to go to the ER, and the house was still standing when we got back.

* * *

"I'm nervous as hell 'bout this class. Maybe we should turn around and cancel," I blurted out.

Major and I were on our way to the Breathless class. Miss Stevenson had been impressed with our progress since we started with her and let us in two weeks early.

We really worked hard at finding ourselves again. I even

came up with a schedule that allowed us to carve out one date night every two weeks. Major's mom actually agreed to watch the kids as long as it was on the same night Sienna and Savior chose. My nephews helped to keep the girls occupied, which was why she changed her mind.

It felt like old times, hanging out with my sister and her husband. When Sienna and I first met Major and Savior, we did everything together. Our asses would drink and dance all night long, into the wee hours of the morning. Now, we were in bed by nine, watching repeats of *Martin*.

"Yeah, right. Shit, we need this class," Major responded, stopping at the red light.

"And what's that supposed to mean, nigga?" I questioned, feeling insulted.

"Stop bein' defensive. You already know I love how you put it down. All I'm sayin' is, it won't hurt to learn somethin' new or improve on what we already know." I looked over at him. "And I'm speakin' 'bout me, not you."

He cleaned that up quickly after my eyes burned a hole in the side of his head. When the light turned green, Major pulled off and continued to head to the address Miss Stevenson gave us. Her studio where she taught the class wasn't that far from her office.

Once we arrived, Major parked, killed the engine, and exited the truck. He walked around to my side and opened the door.

"Thank you, babe." I smiled.

The studio was in a plaza with other businesses. It was still light out, so you were able to see the address on the building. I wasn't too sure if we would have seen it in the dark. The shit looked like someone wrote the numbers on it with a marker, and the business name wasn't written on it either.

"You welcome. I hope it's the right place. This shit looks weird as hell."

"Push the bell. If she doesn't answer, we're outta here." I crossed my arms across my chest and waited.

Before Major could make it all the way to the door, Miss Stevenson swung it open. I almost didn't recognize her. She had her hair out, and it was down her back. Normally she had it pulled back into a bun. The form fitting, cranberry colored pants suit Miss Stevenson wore revealed all the curves she usually had hidden away.

Her glasses had been traded in for a pair of contacts that made her light brown eyes sparkle. Whoever did Miss Stevenson's makeup gave her a natural beat that enhanced a beauty that didn't really require much help.

"Well, hello," she greeted us.

"Good evening," I replied, amazed.

Major must have been just as mesmerized by her transformation as I was. He stood there, speechless, with his tongue almost hanging out. I had to pluck him on the ear to remind his ass I was standing behind him. This muthafucka cleared his throat before speaking.

"Umm, hello to you too."

"Please come in." She held the door open for us.

"Don't get fucked up."

I whispered in Major's ear once we made it inside. He gave

me a stupid grin and put his hand on the small of my back, ushering me forward. Miss Stevenson led us to a room in the back that looked like a lounge area inside of a club. From the appearance of the building outside, I was shocked by the decor on the inside. It definitely was night and day.

"Sit down and get comfortable." We sat on the plush, L-shaped sectional while Miss Stevenson walked over to a bar that was off to the side. It was fully stocked. She fixed herself a drink. "Can I offer you guys something to sip on?"

"Hennessy and ginger ale for the both of us. Thanks," Major answered.

He knew what I liked, and that was one of our favorite drinks. Sienna and Savior watched the girls and said they could stay the night since it was the weekend, so we were able to indulge.

Miss Stevenson gave us our glasses, then grabbed a director's chair that was sitting off to the side and pulled it to the center of the room. Her vibe was totally relaxed and completely different from when she was in her office. She took a seat in front of us and crossed her legs.

"Welcome to Breathless. I want to reintroduce myself. Here, you can refer to me as Strawberry. Miss Stevenson doesn't exist in this realm. If you're wondering why I chose that name it's because a strawberry is sweet, juicy, succulent, and considered an aphrodisiac, especially when it's covered in chocolate.

"When you bite into a plump, ripe strawberry, the juices run down your hands as you enjoy the only fruit with the seeds on the outside. You lick the sweet liquid off your fingers and lips before going in for another taste. It's the food of love, which I want you to have plenty of. "

Miss Stevenson's, I mean Strawberry's, voice was so damn sexy as she spoke. Her facial expressions matched the smooth and silky tone. No one has ever made a strawberry sound so damn sexual. This bitch was making me wet, and I don't bat for the other team, but at this moment I almost forgot that. The way she stared into my eyes as she described the fruit almost put me in a trance.

When I looked over at Major, he licked his lips and let out a deep breath. He was aroused as well. The atmosphere, which was very relaxing, didn't help either. She had the lights down low, and it smelled like peaches and cream candles were burning, but I didn't see any. The mood was definitely set. If this was part of her plan, she definitely knew what the hell she was doing.

I was so turned on that I was ready to fuck my husband as she watched. When Major reached over and placed his hand on my thigh, I knew he felt the same way.

Chapter Eight

MAJOR

W*oah, tiger, not right now.*

I had to talk to my dick in order to calm him down. He became aroused from the way Strawberry spoke of the little, red fruit. She focused on Mecca while talking, and it had me wondering if she wanted to taste her strawberry, and that was what got me excited.

It took everything in me not to strip Mecca down to nothing and eat her pussy while Strawberry watched. The thought of fucking my wife in front of others never crossed my mind until this very moment. Now I understood why people enjoyed wild orgies. Watching a porno didn't give me the same thrill I now felt at the thought of having someone else in the same room with us while we enjoyed each other.

Before having kids, Mecca and I used to watch pornos all

the time. We would try to do the shit we saw and become extra aroused seeing and hearing people have sex. After tonight, we might have to go back to that.

"How did you two feel while I was describing why I chose my name? Let's start with Mecca."

Miss Stevenson focused her attention on my wife, which caused her to blush.

"Well, I was a lil turned on to be honest, and I'll never look at a strawberry the same way again."

When Mecca smiled after giving her response, Strawberry ran her tongue across her top lip. If I didn't know any better, I would say she wanted to fuck my wife. The way her eyes were trained on Mecca, you would think Strawberry was ready to risk it all.

"I felt the same way and wanted to take it a step further."

"And by taking it a step further, do you mean you wanted to fuck your wife? Did you want to rip her clothes off, pick her up, and sit her pussy on your face while I watched? Did you want to make her sweet nectar drip down your fingers and imagine it was the juice from a strawberry as you slopped it up? Did you want to turn her over and slap her ass with your dick before sliding it into her tight opening and pound away?"

Strawberry's response was wild. Miss Stevenson was definitely not in the building. Her alter ego was running this class.

"Yeah, I did. And I'm gone need you to stay up outta my head." I laughed.

"That's my job. To know what you are thinking by the way your body reacts to what is being said or seen. The whole purpose of this class is to teach you both how to leave each other breathless. This is a three week course that is broken down into three parts. You can't have sex during this time. All—"

"Hold up... I'm sure I didn't hear you right. You might wanna run that by me again."

I interrupted Strawberry because she just said some bullshit.

"You heard me correctly. Three weeks may seem like a long time, but it's not. It's all about having self control," she reasoned.

"That's easy for you to say. We just started fuckin' in our own bed and not in the back of Mecca's mail truck or the bathroom for five minutes, and now you want us to stop? Nah, bruh."

I kissed my teeth and leaned forward, resting my elbows on my knees. This was crazy, and I didn't sign up for this shit.

"You know that saying, absence makes the heart grow fonder? In this case, the heart is Mecca's pussy. Even though she has a duty to please you as well, the responsibility falls on you at the end of the day as a man. If you can get attuned with her body and learn everything that makes it tick, Mecca will submit to your every demand sexually. You will have complete control, and she will be more than happy to please you back. Right now, you're just focused on the act and having an orgasm.

"I guarantee you she just plays along half the time because she's not aroused, which is why she didn't make having sex with you a priority before y'all started counseling. She's tired and has a million things on her mind when it comes to the kids and the household, so she's not focused. Abstaining from intercourse will help you and Mecca focus on what you need to work on."

I looked over at Mecca to see her reaction to Strawberry's words and guilt was written all over her face.

"You fakin' it, Mecca?" I quizzed.

"No, I've never faked an orgasm wit' you... but I may have exaggerated how good it felt a time or two. I know it helps you cum faster when you hear me moaning and groaning. Sometimes I'm just not into it, but that's on me," she confessed.

I felt embarrassed and betrayed. All this time I thought the only issue with our sex life was making time for it, but to learn it was the sex itself was a blow to my ego.

"Major, I can tell by your reaction you feel a way. From getting to know you guys, Mecca isn't rushing you to finish because you're doing a bad job. She's tired and drained but loves you enough to want to make sure you're still pleased," Strawberry explained.

"That's what I meant, babe. I just didn't communicate it properly, and I'm sorry. Sometimes I wanna go straight to sleep after my shower, and you don't. We worked hard gettin' the girls to sleep in their own bed, so I wanna make sure I still do my part as your wife."

"And sex can get boring and seem routine when you've been together a long time. It's been ten years of the same dick and pussy for y'all, with a lifetime to go. You have to switch it up, and that's where I come in at. Breathless consists of three parts: mental stimulation, verbal stimulation, and physical stimulation. In order to achieve this sexual trinity, a certain level of intimacy must be achieved. You guys know how to fuck but have no idea how to be intimate with each other. During this first week, it's all about Mecca. Major, you will learn how to mentally stimulate your wife."

Strawberry took a sip from her drink that was sitting in the cup holder attached to her chair.

"I like the sound of that," Mecca cooed, rubbing her hand across my back. I wanted to pluck the shit out of her.

"You will learn to make love to her mind. Men usually cum all the time during sex, but it's not always the case for us women. We need to be mentally aroused as well. The mistake most men make is thinking this only takes place during the course of the physical act, but that's not true. It starts the minute you wake up. Do you guys get up at the same time each day?" Strawberry inquired.

"I'm usually up first because I have to get all three girls ready in the morning, so I like to have some time for myself before wakin' 'em up. I also make breakfast for all of us, pack up the girls' snacks and if it's a Monday, I have to bring their blankets and extra clothes for the week."

Hearing Mecca describe her mornings had me in my feelings. My ass slept peacefully while she was up making sure our home ran like a well oiled machine. I never really gave much thought to all she did before our day even started.

"Why don't you get up with Mecca and help her out?" Strawberry stared at me.

"She never asked for my help." I felt attacked.

"And she never will, but that's not what I asked you.

Instead of you answering my question and taking accountability, you pointed the blame at Mecca. I'm not being hard on you, Major. I just want you to see how you can improve. If you were to get up with her, it would cut the time she has to spend on doing everything in half. That would allow you guys some time alone. You can cuddle on the couch with a cup of coffee and watch the news together. When was the last time you did that?"

"As much as I hate to admit it, you right. Mecca always has everything done by the time I get out of the shower." I shook my head.

"If you help her, you can take a shower together. All these things get her juices flowing. She'll be at work thinking about how your hands caressed her body as the water dripped down in between her ass cheeks while you fondled her titties. This is mental stimulation and gets her kitty cat purring. Send a nasty text or a dick pic to her at lunch time. Leave work early one day and pick up the kids, so she can have some time to herself and enjoy the ride home from work in peace, like you do every day."

"Ain't that the truth," Mecca chimed in.

"You'll never have to keep saying how much you love her because your actions will say it all. Try it and see what happens. She'll be ready to bust it wide open for you each and every night. Tomorrow, I want you to get up with Mecca and help without saying anything to her. After you are done, take your wife by the hand and lead her to the shower. Wash her up then get on your knees and put Mecca's pussy in your face. Let's demonstrate exactly what I mean, so you don't fuck it up."

Strawberry finished up her drink before standing to her feet. Mecca and I stood up as well. She had us face each other.

"Major, get down on your knees, grab Mecca's ass, and push her pussy into your face. Let y'all lips touch. Smell it, feel it, but whatever you do, don't lick it. Oral sex is also out of the question until your three weeks are up. Mecca, rub his head, his ears, and his face while he visually takes you all in. This is all part of foreplay, which is very important and something most men don't take their time doing or do it right. Foreplay is also mental stimulation for your wife."

Mecca had on some black leggings, and I wanted to eat her pussy right through the material. Once again, I had to talk my man down. He was ready to brick up and hammer away.

"Okay, Major, you can stand up. Take Mecca's hands and stare into her eyes. When was the last time you stopped to admire her beauty? When was the last time you softly caressed her cheek before pressing your lips against hers? It's probably been a minute because you only focus on fucking. You need to learn how to carve out time to stop and smell the roses and in this case, the pussy. It's all about mentally stimulating Mecca this week, so say or do whatever you have to in order to make her feel like she is the only woman in this world. Let's practice right now."

I watched as a smile creeped across Mecca's beautiful face.

"You are my better half. If it wasn't for you, I don't know—"

"A'ight, that ain't gone work. Mecca doesn't want to hear

what she already knows. Tell her something to make her pussy gain a pulse and start to drip. Here, trade places with me."

Strawberry grabbed Mecca's hands while I stood next to them and watched.

"Staring into your dark, brown eyes is like looking into your soul. Seeing the slight dimple in your left cheek whenever you smile makes me brick up. I can't wait to kiss both of your lips tonight. As soon as we get home I'm gonna strip you naked, put you in the shower, and wash every part of your body. After I take you out and lay you across the bed, I will rub you down with body oil to get that smooth, cocoa brown skin of yours warmed up. Then I'm gonna slide my dick into your tight pussy and fuck you until I watch your soul leave your body and come back. I won't stop until your sweet peach bust open and cream all over me."

Strawberry talked in a soft tone, just above a whisper, and made sure her words were slow and deliberate. She never took her eyes off of Mecca and rubbed her hands as she said some shit you only read in romance books.

"Whew, damn." Mecca fanned herself.

"Listen, we gone have to start the three weeks of no sex tomorrow. I need to take my wife home and practice what we just learned," I informed Strawberry.

She definitely knew what she was doing when it came to teaching people how to put the spice back in their bedroom.

"Well, I guess that's fair, since I didn't inform you ahead of time. But at the stroke of midnight, it's over."

"Okay, so we better get goin'," Mecca announced.

"I'll see you guys here at the same time next week. And before I forget to tell you, we need to check in each night. It will be a five minute zoom call just to make sure you guys are good. Let's say around seven. If something comes up, just let me know."

We finished up our drinks and exited the building.

"Do you think the every night zoom call is too much?" Mecca questioned as we hopped into the truck.

"Hell no. As much as she's charging for this damn class, her muthafuckin' ass needs to come over and tuck us in at night." I started the engine and pulled off.

"Yeah, charging $1,000 for three weeks is nasty work. I've never been turned on by a woman before, though, so I guess she's worth every damn penny 'cause I can't wait to get home and put my pussy in yo face."

Mecca bit her bottom lip as she slid her hand over and started massaging my dick. I stepped on the gas and did the dash all the way home.

Chapter Nine

MECCA

"You guys survived the first week. How do you feel?" Strawberry questioned.

Major and I were back in the Breathless class.

"It was extremely hard not to go all the way, but I feel like Mecca and I are doin' great. I've definitely been takin' a lot of cold showers, though." Major laughed.

"I can genuinely say my husband made me a priority, like he used to before we were married and had kids. This week I wasn't just his wife and the mother of his kids, I was his lover. He made me feel feminine as hell. His words spoke to my soul. This was the Major I missed." I smiled.

The level of attentiveness Major showed me this past week was over and beyond what I thought he would do. He wrote me a note every morning and stuck it to the bathroom mirror, so it was the first thing I saw when I got up. During the day he texted me screenshots of quotes he must have found on social media, but they expressed how he felt about me.

A couple dick pics and raunchy words made their way to my inbox as well. By day three, I had to wear a pantliner because this nigga had my pussy secreting the goodness on a regular. One day I had to place a frozen water bottle between my legs to put my bottom lips on chill because Major had sent over a video we made during the first year of our relationship.

I totally forgot he even recorded us. It was Valentine's Day, and he rented us a room in one of those themed motels. The shit was called the jungle room, and our asses turned into wild animals. We licked, sucked, and fucked all over that damn suite. Major tore the frame out of the bed and my ass. He made my body feel things it never felt before. That was definitely a breathless moment.

When relationships are new, you go all out and have the best of times. You can't get enough of each other, then everything changes as life starts lifing. Nothing should change, but it does because your responsibilities have and now little people who you created need the majority of your time. The bills hit different, and your focus was no longer on each other, but everything else. So watching the younger versions of ourselves be unhinged, without a care in the world, turned me on like never before.

"That's amazing to hear because this week, he's going to become your priority. Verbal stimulation is very important to both people involved, especially the man. He needs to hear that you want him, need him, and value him. It fuels their ego and actually makes them better men. Major wanted you to stop working and be more attentive to his needs because he felt ignored and neglected. You refused and explained to him why working was important for you. I want you to do the same thing when it comes to your sex life.

"Let your husband know what you want. Teach him how to leave you breathless by talking him through it. Men want to know they're the best you ever had. Tell him that, but you have to mean it when you do. He can't be the best if he's not giving you his best. You have to verbally guide him. When you both find the time to get it in, what happens once you're finished? Do you roll over and fall asleep? Do you hop up and go pee and clean yourself up? Or do you lay there, staring at the ceiling, trying to catch your breath as you bask in the glow of the remnants of your love making? If it's not the latter, Mecca, you in danger, girl."

Strawberry poked fun at me using the popular line from the movie *Ghost*. The part when Whoopi Goldberg's character, Oda Mae Brown, was talking to Molly. She sat next to us on the chaise lounge part of the couch wearing an all white catsuit, like the one Toni Braxton wore in the video she did for "You're Makin' Me High".

"Major usually gets me a warm rag, so I can clean myself up. We used to cuddle as I laid my head on his chest but now, I like to stretch out and need my space. The night we left here after the first class was the first time he spooned me in a long time.

Since we couldn't have sex I put Pandora on, and we fell asleep as he held me in his arms. It felt good."

I reached over and rubbed Major's hand, causing him to smile.

"Why do women get all excited to put a warm cloth on their pussy?" Strawberry questioned.

"I guess it's the fact that they go and get it for you. It's thoughtful, you know." I shrugged my shoulders.

"No, I don't know. Put some wipes in a wipe warmer on your nightstand. It works just as well. I rather him scoop you up and put your ass in a warm bubble bath then climb in, so round two can get started. It's the elevation in his determination to satisfy you that will leave you breathless. You guys need to switch it up, but you have to communicate that to him. Wouldn't you rather have a bubble bath than a crusty ass, wet rag?" Strawberry stared at me.

"Of course I would," I replied.

"Then why haven't you told him this? As women we have to speak up because we know what we want. Don't be afraid to tell him to move a lil to the left, stay right there, do that again, or to slow down. If he goes too slow, let him know he needs to pick up the speed. Most importantly, let him know if he is doing something wrong. How can he do better if he doesn't know what to work on? Silence can be deadly for your love life. Before you know it, you will be down to having sex three to four times a month instead of every week because it's not worth the effort."

Strawberry hit the nail on the head. Before we started counseling, when we did sneak it in, it definitely was only a few times throughout the month. It's wild because you don't even know when it started slowing down. You just wake up one day and find yourself in a situation you swore your ass would never be in.

"I don't want to hurt his feelings. It's not like I don't enjoy the time we share. And if I were to say somethin' to him, and this nigga might talk to me crazy, then we gone end up fightin'. No one wants to be told they can't fuck."

"I can't fuck?" Major blurted out.

"When did I say that?" I turned my head to face him.

"Just now, shit."

"Major, she worded it wrong. What she is trying to say is, no one wants to be criticized on how they perform sexually." Strawberry explained it better than I did.

"That's not what the fuck I heard." Major blew his breath.

"See, if we were home and didn't have you as a mediator, this would have gone all the way left. I wasn't even tryna be smart or hurt his feelings. The same could be said for me. I don't wanna be criticized either or told my pussy ain't up to par."

"And this is why I'm going to teach you how to express yourself without insulting him. Major, you also have to be open to hearing what you can improve on. The same goes for Mecca, and we'll get to that during our last week. Right now, we are focusing on her communicating to you. If you allow her to freely express what she likes, and you do exactly what she says, the reward will be great. Her body will respond to you like never before. Let's demonstrate. Mecca, tell him what you want him to do when he's eating your pussy."

Strawberry was so blunt and raw with her words. There was no way in hell she didn't have men, and women, lined up around the corner to get a taste of her. She knew everything about how to please you and had the body of a goddess.

"Umm, well. What do I say? This is awkward as hell."

"Alright, I'll tell him, and you stop me if I say something you wouldn't have said. Okay?"

"Yes." I shook my head as I replied.

Strawberry got up and sat directly next to Major, putting him in the middle of us. She grabbed his hands and stared into his eyes.

"Babe, when you put your mouth in between my legs and are getting ready to devour my pussy, I want you to start by slowly licking and sucking on the insides of my thighs. Spread my legs wide open and give my bottom lips a kiss, then gently rub the tip of your tongue up and down the length of my pussy. Stick it in and out of my opening like you are fucking me, then find your way to my clit.

"I want you to take your time licking all around it. When it begins to swell and its hood comes off, gently suck on it. Flicker your tongue back and forth until you make my juices flow and drip down the crack of my ass. Bury your face in it as I lift my hips and push my pussy further into your mouth. Flatten out your tongue as I grind my hips, creating friction between it and my clit.

"As I moan and call out your name because I can feel my

body heating up and a tingling sensation throughout, stop. Turn me over, slide your dick into my pussy, and fuck me as hard as you can. Don't stop until I shake and shiver beneath you while my pussy muscle puts your dick in a chokehold."

This bitch did it again. She had me ready to hike up the free flowing skirt I had on and sit my pussy on Major's face.

Strawberry looked over at me, winked, then licked her lips as she let his hands go and sat back in her seat.

What the fuck was that?

At first I thought she wore a catsuit to turn Major on but now, I wasn't too sure. He kept saying Strawberry had a thing for me, but I didn't believe him. Her actions just now may have proved Major was right. Even during the zoom calls she focused all of her attention on me. If she did find me appetizing, I guess it could be considered flattering, but I'm strictly dickly.

"You damn sure didn't say anything wrong," I informed Strawberry.

"Major, do you feel you already do everything I just said?"

"For the most part. I guess I could slow down, though. She likes sloppy head and always cums, so I didn't think I was doin' it wrong," he expressed.

"You're not doing it wrong... the technique needs to be elevated, though. And Mecca cums because she's being physically simulated. Clitorial stimulation is the easiest way for a woman to experience an orgasm. The point isn't to just make her reach her peak. You want to leave her breathless. Mecca should be shaking like a leaf in a windstorm, gasping for air, and ready to kill a bitch if she looks your way once she climaxes.

"There's levels to the type of orgasms she can achieve, and you want hers to be explosive. Why give her the experience of a lonely wave crashing onto the sand when you can give her a tsunami? They're caused by earthquakes or volcanic eruptions under the sea. Mecca's pussy is the sea you explore, and she wants you to go deep sea diving in order to snatch the pearl from her clam whenever you step foot on the beach."

I leaned over and gave Major a kiss.

"You ready to put yo scuba gear on once this class is finished, babe?" He smiled.

"That's what I want to see, Mecca. Encourage your man. Do you call or text Major during the day to let him know you're thinking about him? Once he steps foot in the door from work, do you inquire about his day or just complain about yours? When was the last time you told him what an amazing husband and father he is? Do you pray for him or with him? Have you ever taken him out on a date?"

Strawberry kept firing off all these questions at me, and I felt like the tables had turned. Last week Major was in the hot seat. Now, it was my turn, and I didn't like it.

"No, complain, it's been a minute, yes, and no."

I cut my eyes once I answered all her questions.

"Why do you look pissed at me? These questions aren't designed to get under your skin. I ask them in order for you to see where you can improve. Major had to put in the work, so the same goes for you. Speak life into your husband and watch him become puddy in your hands. All this week I want you to verbally stimulate Major.

"Leave him voicemails on his work phone. Send voice messages to his cell. Take five minutes out of your day to tell the man who wants nothing more in this life but to make you happy how you feel about him. Couples make the mistake of getting comfortable. They forget to keep doing the same things they did before marriage and kids."

"That's so true," I agreed, reluctantly. "Major and I used to talk on the phone for hours when we first met. I can't tell you how many times I fell asleep on the phone 'cause I didn't want to be the first one to hang up."

"You mean snored into the phone." Major laughed. "And when I said somethin', you tried to act like you weren't sleep. Then we'd end up talkin' 'til the sun came up 'bout nothin'."

"Look at the smiles on both y'all faces. This is what I want to see all the time. Now, let's talk about your final week. I want to discuss it now because we will have a lot to work on to get you guys ready, so I want to get the details of your last night out of the way. You will take everything you learned about mental and verbal stimulation and apply it when doing the physical stimulation.

"I will email you a video I made showing you different sexual positions you can try. These are not your normal positions that most couples do. They're very explicit, visually and verbally, so make sure you watch them once the kids are asleep. I want y'all to get your bodies ready for the finale, which will take place at a five star hotel I have reserved for you, but practice with your clothes on.

"Mecca, on that day, I want you to leave voice messages for

Major from the moment he gets up until it's time for him to meet you at the hotel. He won't have any prior information of the location, only you. I will work with you that week on zoom, during your lunch hour, on what you will say to him. If y'all can stay at different locations the night before, it will make this a lot more fun.

"He will arrive first. The key to the room will be waiting for him at the front desk, along with a basket of pleasurable goodies. You will arrive at the hotel around an hour later in order to make sure he has time to follow all your instructions. I want you to dress like a classy whore. It will be like a role play date. He's the client, you are the trick, and I'm the pimp. I'm so excited for you both."

This class was worth every dollar we paid her.

"Sounds good. I wasn't expectin' it to end like that. We can't thank you enough," Major expressed.

"No need to thank me. I love what I do and couples like you make my job fun and easy. Just make sure to leave me a good yelp review." Strawberry laughed.

I had my guard up in the beginning, but she turned out to be a great help to Major and I. Too bad Savior and Sienna didn't have the same experience as we did. They would have enjoyed this class.

Chapter Ten

MAJOR

"Welcome to your last week in the Breathless master class. This is the one all couples get excited for, physical stimulation."

Strawberry spoke to Mecca and I wearing an outfit that left nothing to the imagination. If it wasn't for the pasties covering her nipples and the thong up her ass, she would have been completely naked under the sheer, red dress she wore. She had us sit at the bar tonight as she played bartender.

"I'm definitely excited. I can't wait until we actually get to put everythin' we learned into action. The way Major responded to me tellin' him how much I loved and wanted him made me feel good. Because of this class, I realize how important it is to make that part of my regular communication with him. One night, he left me a note on the bed to meet him outside after we put the kids down. It turned out to be an invitation to have a picnic under the stars. He had small, individual wine bottles for us, some grapes, cheese, and crackers."

"Mental and visual stimulation. Nice, Major," Strawberry complimented.

"As we laid on the blanket, staring at the stars and holding hands, I told Major how much he meant to me and how my life was so much better with him in it. Then I explained what he needed to do to me when we finally got the chance to go all the way again, which got us all hot and bothered."

"Look at my star pupils putting in that work." Strawberry clapped her hands. "Yes, Mecca. That's a perfect segue into what we will be discussing tonight. When y'all held hands while freely expressing your emotions, there was a transfer of energy. Major not only heard what you said, but he felt it. Our bodies are made up of energy, so we have to be mindful of how we share it, especially when it comes to the physical act of love making.

"When our bodies are connected, energy is transferred. Sex is one of the most powerful exchanges of energy as humans. We can heal or even harm each other if we aren't careful. This is why I wanted you guys to work on your mental and verbal stimulation before being physical again. You drain each other's energy when you're not on the same page, which was why Major was dissatisfied when you two weren't fucking on the regular."

"Well, damn. You be spittin' some real shit." I took a sip from the drink she made us. It was our usual.

"That's what you pay me the big bucks for. I've done my research and experience is always the best teacher. My life was hard, and I was forced to grow up fast. One of the reasons I went into counseling was because I wanted to help people. Everyone deserves to be loved correctly. When you commit to spending a lifetime together, you have to always remember the little things, like a hug. When was the last time you held Mecca in your embrace for longer than three seconds?"

"I do hug her, here and there, but it's not like we embrace for a long time. It's quick," I admitted.

"Your wife doesn't deserve a church hug. She needs to feel your weight against her body. You want her to know she is safe in your arms, cared for, and loved. A hug will evoke all those emotions. I want you, right now, to hug Mecca like it's your second date, and you haven't taken a sip from her golden flower. You know how you guys are, trying to get a quick feel by hugging. I bet you hugged her all the time before she gave you a taste."

"Yup, he did." Mecca laughed.

We stood up, and I pulled her into me and squeezed tight. Mecca wrapped her arms around my waist and laid her head on my chest.

"This feels good," Mecca expressed.

"Take in her scent, Major. Rub her back. Massage her ass while whispering in her ear how you can't wait to suck on her titties and eat her pussy. Make this woman, who's willing to suck your dick while rubbing your nutsack, blush." We all laughed. "See, find someone you can laugh with, and you won't be sad a day in your life."

"I can stay like this forever," Mecca cooed.

"Well, not right now. Let him go because I have some things I want to show y'all before it gets too late, but I want y'all to hug at least twice a day from now on. Meet me over by the couch after you finish your drink," Strawberry instructed.

Mecca and I downed the Hennesy and ginger ale, then made our way over to the couch.

"I hope this is a hands-on exercise." I laughed but was serious.

"It definitely is. I want to show you different sex positions you can do on a couch that y'all probably didn't think of, with you both taking turns being in control."

For the rest of the night, Strawberry showed us things I would have never thought to do. Mecca and I hung onto her every word and watched in amazement as she demonstrated different moves. Our date night couldn't come fast enough.

"Be at the hotel across the street from the building with the gold roof in an hour. When you get in the room, take a shower. Wrap yourself up in a towel and wait for that dick to be devoured. I won't be long because I'm on my way. My pussy has been yearning for this moment all day. It's ready to be slapped, plucked, and licked like never before. Are you ready for me to be your little whore?"

I was listening to the voice message Mecca sent me. She had been talking to me like this all day. The week flew by, and it was finally time for us to enjoy our date night. In a way, I was glad we had to wait. It forced us to learn about each other on a deeper level and forced us to open up in ways we never would have before. Our conversations had become very transparent, and neither of us held back.

Mecca actually stayed at Sienna and Savior's house with the kids last night. We owed them big time for helping us out over the course of the three weeks. My anticipation of seeing my wife later today was definitely heightened by her not being around.

As I packed a duffel bag, I thought of how lucky I was to have found a woman like Mecca. She held no punches, and her heart was pure. In this life I believe you only get one true love, and Mecca was mine.

Once I had everything together, I jumped in my truck and headed out early. The hotel she referenced was thirty minutes from where we lived. If I ran into traffic, it would take me even longer. This was one engagement I didn't want to be late for.

When I arrived at the hotel, I valet parked and walked inside. It gave off a very rich vibe and most of the guests walking about were much older than I expected. Strawberry said all I had to do was find the front desk associate with red hair pulled into a ponytail at the counter. She had already reserved the room, so I didn't need to do anything but show her my ID.

I spotted the young woman right away and walked over to her. She looked at my license to make sure it was me and had a sly grin on her face when she passed me the gift basket that

Strawberry left for us. The items inside were visible through the clear, cellophane wrap and didn't leave anything to the imagination. All the items looked like they came from a BDSM sex shop.

After getting the keycard to the suite, I headed toward the elevators and stepped inside. People stared at me, and some even giggled, as they admired the contents of the oversized basket on our ride up. When I made it to my floor, I stepped off and found the room. It was nestled in the corner away from the elevators.

Imagine my surprise to see a trail of red, rose petals when I opened the door. They led me straight to the master bedroom with a king size bed, which had a phone setup on a tripod at the end of it. This was definitely unexpected.

"Oh, we gettin' freaky, freaky tonight," I said out loud, sitting the basket on the dresser across from the bed and my duffel bag on the floor beside it.

Mecca mentioned she enjoyed the old video I sent of us. I guess she wanted to create a new one. Obviously Strawberry must have helped or gave Mecca early access to the room to set it up.

Excited, I quickly made my way to the master bathroom and stripped out of my clothes to take a shower. There was a note on the mirror, like the ones I left Mecca during the first week of our class. The note was written in her handwriting, so she definitely was here. It had instructions for me to go into the top, right drawer of the dresser after my shower and retrieve the items in it.

After showering, I dried off and wrapped the towel around my waist. When I went back into the room and opened the dresser drawer, there was another note laying on a black eye mask. It instructed me to put the mask on after laying down in the middle of the bed. Mecca also wrote down what she planned on doing as soon as she walked in. I don't know what the hell Strawberry taught her during their zoom meetings this past week, but I damn sure loved the vulgarness of Mecca's words.

The curtains were already drawn, but the sunlight still creeped through a little, adding to the ambiance of the room. After laying down and putting the mask over my eyes, I thought about all the nasty shit Mecca and I was about to do. The video Strawberry sent us to watch was etched into my brain, and I planned on trying every position.

I heard the lock on the door click as it opened and closed, then the chain lock went on. Hearing the sounds cleared my thoughts, and my dick immediately started to come alive underneath the towel. Mecca was early. The anticipation must have gotten to her as well.

"Hey, babe, I hope you haven't been waitin' too long."

Mecca's voice sounded far away, but sexy as hell. She must have been in the doorway. Not being able to see her added to the mystery of the whole situation.

"Nah, you right on time," I yelled out.

The scent of her favorite perfume danced in the air, letting me know she was now standing close to me. When she let her fingers slowly slide up my leg and removed the towel, my dick was now at full attention.

"I see someone is happy to see me," Mecca cooed.

"You damn straight. I'm jealous that he has his eye on you, and I don't." I laughed.

"Just lay back and get ready to be sucked and fucked like never before after I start this video."

I got goosebumps hearing my wife's sultry voice. She wasn't wasting any time. Mecca must have grabbed the basket because I could hear the crunching of the cellophane wrap.

The next thing I knew, she put handcuffs on my right wrist and pulled my arm up. I wondered what the hell she was going to cuff it to, but then I remembered the headboard was one of those wall mounted, floating ones that had a bar across it.

After securing my wrist to it, she came around to the other side of the bed and did the same thing to my left one. We only used handcuffs once before, and vowed never to do it again because Mecca left the damn key at home when we went away one weekend. I was never so embarrassed. A staff member at the lodge had to come over to the cabin we were in and cut me loose.

"I hope you remembered the keys this time," I joked.

"Shhhhhh," was her only response.

Mecca put on some music. She had it turned up loud as hell too. I guess she wanted to drown out the sounds we were about to make.

A few seconds later, I felt warm oil come in contact with my skin. Mecca started with my feet and slowly worked her way up my legs, making sure she didn't miss a spot. My dick started throbbing and waving for attention.

When she pushed my legs far apart, I felt a way. Usually Mecca would get on her knees and position herself on the side of me, so I could massage her ass and pussy while she pleased me. This time I was spread eagle, in a feminine way, and had to catch myself from kneeing her ass.

"This is diff—" Mecca placed her lips on the head of my dick, cutting me off.

She sucked on it and traced the rim with her tongue, then swallowed me whole. My toes curled, and the hairs on the back of my neck stood up. When she tickled my balls with the tip of her tongue as she deepthroated me, I was left breathless. Mecca had never done that before.

"Ahhhhhh," I moaned like a bitch and didn't care.

The way my wife was working me over had my stomach muscles contracting. Mecca always made me feel great, but this time she definitely elevated her determination to please me. Strawberry must have given her private lessons or sent her some videos on it, separately, because her technique was top notch.

Even when I felt like I was about to bust in her mouth, about five minutes into it, she immediately stopped sucking. Mecca gripped my dick at the base and firmly squeezed. Once I let out a deep breath, she resumed slurping and sucking like a champ. We did this a few times over a course of what felt like forever.

I was experiencing a whole new side of my wife this evening. We might have to sign up for an extended class. If this was just the appetizer, I couldn't wait for the main course. When I finally erupted in her mouth, my body jerked uncontrollably. All I wanted to do at that moment was please my wife in the same way she just blessed me.

"How did that feel, babe?" Mecca quizzed.

"Indescribable. You definitely did yo big one, goddamn," I complimented.

"Well, now it's time for me to sit my pussy on yo face and let you eat 'til you're full."

When she lowered her pussy onto my mouth, I immediately knew something was wrong. The person in the room with me sounded like Mecca, smelled like Mecca, but she wasn't Mecca. I was in the most compromising position of my life, being blind folded, handcuffed, and in a hotel room with a strange woman, but I would be damned if it went any further.

Without giving it a second thought, I took a bite out of crime. When my teeth chomp down on the pussy lips of whoever was on top of me, she screamed out.

"Ughhhhh, you stupid muthafucka!"

I recognized that voice right away. It was Strawberry's dirty ass.

Chapter Eleven

STRAWBERRY

"I can't believe you just bit me like that. What the fuck is wrong wit' cho ass?" I barked, hopping up and off the bed.

"You crazy ass bitch. Uncuff me right now, so I can fuck you up," he threatened.

Major tried his hardest to free himself, but he wasn't going anywhere.

"You ain't gone do shit, nigga." I felt in between my legs and when I looked at my fingers, they had traces of my blood on them. "Muthafucka!"

Pissed, I ran over and slapped the shit out of Major, and snatched the mask off his face.

"As soon as I get loose, Imma dunk yo ass right on yo head." He kicked his feet and almost connected, but I moved out of the way just in time. "Who the fuck are you for real? All that proper speakin' you did in counselin' went right out the window, huh? Stankin' ass gutter rat."

"Fuck you! I can't believe I started falling for yo raggedy ass, and compromised everything I worked so hard for. You stupid bitch, Strawberry."

I started pulling my hair and punching myself.

"Oh, you crazy, crazy," Major jeered.

For some reason Major reminded me of my first love, Wess. He was the splitting image of him; down to the way he smiled, the waves in his hair, and even the way he stood. This man even smelled like him. The way he loved Mecca and wanted to give her the world made me jealous and mad at the same time. He was so infatuated with her ass it was sickening.

"And you're gonna be divorced as soon as I send Mecca a clip of the movie we just made. When she sees me sucking on yo dick, she's gonna lose her mind." I laughed. "She won't believe shit you have to say after listening to you moan and groan while I snatched yo soul. And you enjoyed every second of it. No one has ever made you feel like I just did. What is done is done. Even if you do convince her to stay, she'll never forget about today. From now on, whenever Mecca does go down on you, you will always wish it was me."

I stuck my tongue out and wiggled it at him while rubbing on my titties. My pussy was still throbbing from the pain of his bite, but I had to push that to the side right now.

"Yeah, you on drugs for sure. Probably eating bath salts and shit. Mecca knows I wouldn't voluntarily let you put yo nasty ass mouth on me. I don't give a fuck how good it felt in the moment, I will never think of yo miserable, lonely, psychotic ass when I'm wit' my wife. Obviously you wanna be her, but you never will, bitch" Major spewed.

"How did you know I wasn't her anyway?" I questioned.

That was the part that really baffled me. I did everything right, leaving no room for error but the minute I went too far, he knew it wasn't Mecca. If I would have just stuck to the original plan, I wouldn't have fumbled the ball. When I first laid eyes on Major, I knew I had to have a piece of him. The only way that could happen was through the Breathless class, which was a scam.

Normally, a member of my team would meet the husband at the hotel, and she would do everything I just did, minus trying to get her pussy ate. She was just as deadly as me with her mouth and hands. I masturbated to the videos she made. Watching her please all these unexpecting men made my pussy drip. Once he reached his climax, she would uncuff one of his hands.

He thought it was all a part of the act, so he wouldn't be none the wiser on what was going to happen next. Once she had everything packed up, my partner sat the key on the night stand by the hand that was still secure. After telling him to remove the mask, he was surprised to see it wasn't his wife. The husband was then told, with a glock pointing directly at him, not to make a move. She advised him that an email would be sent with an account number to wire $1,000 a month via Western Union for a year. If a payment was missed, the video would be sent to his wife. I made sure to only choose people who could afford the payments and already had a sketchy past. Most would pay the $12,000 out right to be done. Once the payment was complete, the video was destroyed.

After that, she would leave and the spouse would show up on time. They still enjoyed their night, especially since his first nut was already out of the way. I knew this for a fact because the front desk associate that always checked them in, who was the manager of the hotel, was a part of my team as well. She gave me the same room every time and received a cut of the profits. No one ever called down to make a complaint.

Nothing could be traced back to us either because they had to pay cash for the Breathless class. The company didn't exist on paper, so there was nothing to connect me to it. As far as the marriage counseling went, that gig was legit, but all good things must come to an end. I was sure Mecca would want to call the police, Major not so much. He was pissed now, but not enough to go to the authorities and tell them what happened. She might be able to convince him later, though, and I couldn't take that chance by sticking around.

"Mecca always left a landin' strip in the shape of a heart for me. Yo sewer ass pussy was a bald eagle wit' a faint, unpleasant smell. What I wanna know is how the fuck you made yo voice sound like hers?"

I never considered Mecca to have a French wax instead of a Brazilian. That fucking bitch. The fact I didn't get my shit off and probably needed stitches on my pussy because this trick kept a patch on hers enraged me even more.

Time was of the essence, so I had to get out of there, but I wanted to beat the shit out of Major and wait for Mecca to show up and whip her ass too.

"By the end of week two I gained Mecca's trust, which was all part of my plan. You probably thought I was coming on to her, and I was. It was all to get you two fools to believe I wanted her and not you. When we were practicing what she was going to say to yo ass today, I recorded her words. What you heard was the recording I put together to play back to you. We also met up because I needed her to hand write the notes you found. She was so damn happy when I told her I would decorate the room for y'all. Stupid ass."

Major tried to get loose again after I insulted his little wife. Watching him struggle excited me. I grabbed my phone to make a call.

"It's a code red. Don't let the wife in and call Dana to let her know it's time to close up shop. Meet us at the spot in an hour. We leave tonight," I informed Shonda at the front desk.

"You not gonna get away wit' this!"

"I just did, and fucking around with you I probably need a tetanus shot. You can stay cuffed until yo bitch ass wife finds you. Too bad I didn't get a chance to taste her as well. I'm sure that woulda made you blast off like a rocket ship, seeing my juicy lips on her pussy as I made her cum harder than you ever could. It's been a pleasure, though."

Gathering all my belongings, I rushed out of the room and took the service elevator to the basement. Shonda gave me my own key. From there, I exited out of the back door and made my way to my car.

Dana said coming here was a bad idea when I told her what I planned. She knew this was going to end bad because it wasn't the first time I had done something like this. It happened a few years ago in Maryland, which was why we made our way to Jersey. In that situation the wife came back and shot up my office. During our sessions she left out the part where she had a collection of guns and knew how to use them.

I could feel my phone vibrating on my lap as I drove to the meeting spot we had set up for emergencies. Swiping to connect the call, I spoke to Dana through the car.

"Shonda just called me. I told yo ass not to let them do the Breathless class. I'm tired of relocating. This was the best job I had so far, and we had a lot of clients from it. Those people stay havin' issues."

I cut my eyes. She was right, but I didn't want to hear the shit right now. Dana wanted me to just keep them as regular clients. Even when I told her they were definitely doing the Breathless class, she begged me to just end it there and leave the hotel part out, but I had to have things my way.

In my mind, Major would have never told Mecca about what happened between us and took it to his grave. Obviously I was wrong, judging by the way he assaulted me. Ninety-nine percent of the men in his situation would have gone through with it, but not ole faithful.

"Just meet me at the spot. This nigga tried to bite a chunk

out of my pussy lips, so I need you to look at it to make sure it's not infected," I replied.

"What type of freaky deaky shit was y'all on?"

"I'll explain everything later. Right now we have to make all the calls to get shit in order. It's time to say goodbye to Jersey and hello to a new state. Wess will be home soon. Once he's out, we'll settle down for good." I sighed.

"I miss my brother. He damn sure won't be happy when he finds out all the bullshit you been doin'?"

"Who's gonna tell him? I hope not you because, you would have a lot of explaining to do yourself," I informed Dana.

"Well, I'm on my way. Savior has been an excellent boss to me. It's a shame I have to leave him hangin' like this." Dana blew her breath.

"You shoulda fucked him when you had the chance and gave him something to remember you by." I laughed.

"Nah, he loved his wife. I'm sure he liked the view, but that nigga knew to stay on his side of the fence. Don't think I wasn't lookin' for the chance to shoot my shot, though. I tried, but he never took the bait. I'm gonna miss him."

"Oh, please. You always fall for the ones you can never have. These brothers were two of the same. I hate niggas like them. I'll see you soon."

I disconnected the call and pulled over to the side of the road. Since Mecca was going to find out what happened anyway, she might as well see it for herself. The phone on the tripod was mine, and it recorded everything.

After editing the video in small clips, I sent them to her.

Knowing she would be miserable, even if only for a little while, was satisfying enough. These women who didn't appreciate the men they had needed to be taught a lesson.

And if there was one thing I hated more than a weak woman, it was a weak man. They deserved everything they got. I couldn't make them all miserable, but the ones I could I damn sure did. All my life I lived by the motto, get them before they get you.

Pulling back onto the road, I thought about which state I wanted to explore next. Whichever one I chose definitely wouldn't be the same after my arrival. I loved shaking things up.

Chapter Twelve

MECCA

"Hello, my name is Mecca Holland. My husband checked in earlier this evening. The second key to our room should have been left here for me," I informed the front desk associate.

This hotel was really fancy, and I felt out of place standing there in a pink, trench coat dress, completely naked underneath.

"I'm sorry, ma'am, but I don't have a keycard with your name on it. Are you sure it's this hotel?"

The young woman with red hair stared at me. I could tell by her expression she was serious as hell.

"Can you check under my husband's name? It's Major Holland. Strawberry said you would help us, so I'm confused." She laughed.

"Strawberry? I don't know who that is, and there is no one

with the last name Holland in our system. You must have the wrong hotel. Try the one a few miles down the way." She pointed toward the door.

I took a deep breath, trying to calm myself. After pulling out my phone, I looked at the email Strawberry sent me on the location of the hotel. Just to make sure I wasn't bugging and before I completely lost my shit, I walked back outside of the hotel. The building across the street had a gold roof. It was the only building in our area with that color.

With all the strength I could muster, I walked back into the hotel and over to the young woman, who fit the exact description of the front desk associate Strawberry said would give me the extra keycard. She looked like she was packing up her stuff to leave.

"Before you go, can you please double check again for the keycard? Maybe someone misplaced it. I know for a fact my husband came in here about an hour ago and is waiting for me. Strawberry said the room was already reserved, and you would help me."

"Bitch, I said ain't no damn keycard here for you. Now get the fuck up outta my face." She spoke through clenched teeth.

Spinning my head around, I looked to see if anyone else was in my vicinity that this crazy ass bitch could be speaking to. Seeing no one else, I focused my attention back on her.

"I don't know who the fuck you think you talkin' to, but I will jump over this counter and beat all the red outta yo muthafuckin' head. You got me all the way fucked up. Let me speak to a manager," I demanded.

"I'm the manager, so yeah."

She stuck her finger up at me and walked away, causing me to gasp.

"You can't go to jail. There are three lil people who need you."

I spoke out loud to myself. It was the only way to keep my cool because I wanted to beat this Sexyy Red look alike down.

"Is there someone I can speak to?" I asked another worker who was also behind the counter. "The person I was just talkin' to, who claimed to be the manager, was very rude to me. All I want is the keycard to my room."

"She is the manager, so I don't know how much help I'm going to be," he responded.

I didn't want to, but I took out my phone and called my husband. When he didn't answer, I started to get nervous and a sick feeling in the pit of my stomach. When I went to text Strawberry, hoping she had some answers for me, multiple text messages started popping up from her.

Strawberry said she would teach us how to leave each other breathless, and her ass stuck to that promise. When I clicked on the video and saw her and Major together, all the air left my lungs. It felt like an elephant was sitting on my chest. I couldn't breath, yell, or move.

It was as if my feet were in a block of cement, and I was standing in quicksand. Never in my wildest dreams did I ever think Major would disrespect and embarrass me in such a way. I felt like I could die at that very moment. The amount of pressure that quickly collected in my head made me feel weak.

"Are you being helped?"

Hearing the voice of a random stranger, who I assumed wanted me to move, broke me out of the state of shock I was in. I swiftly walked out of the hotel and made my way back to the valet attendant. My car was still out front in the line of other cars waiting to be parked for the night.

"Did you change your mind about staying?"

The same person who originally took my keys questioned me. I shook my head yes. As I stood there like a deer caught in headlights, the tears started to flow.

"Ma'am, are you okay?"

My body felt like it wanted to expel all the hurt I was currently feeling, but I couldn't even scream. Taking slow, deep breaths, I was finally able to speak.

"Please, just give me my keys. I need to go," I informed him.

After getting in my car, I started the engine and drove off. About thirty minutes later, I found myself pulling up to Major's mother's house. My body subconsciously drove me here. She was the only other person I trusted with my heart outside of my twin.

There was no way I could go to Sienna's house right now. My kids didn't need to see me like this, and neither did my nephews. The people responsible for creating me would say all the things I didn't want to hear if I went to their house. They have been waiting for something like this to happen to our relationship, so they could say they tried to warn me.

I also didn't want to be alone, so ending up here was what my soul needed at the moment. The bond I developed with my mother-in-law was one I cherished. She was my diary in human form and always gave me the best advice. Even though she loved her sons with her whole heart, she never chose their side when they were wrong, like most mothers do.

"Mecca! Mecca!"

Bam! Bam!

Momma Peggy, which was what I called her, banged on my window to get my attention as she yelled my name. I was parked outside her house with the car still running.

"I'm sorry, I didn't notice that you came outside," I informed her after rolling down my window.

"I saw you on the camera sitting out here. Once you never came inside, I decided to check on you. What the hell is going on? You look like shit."

My lips began to quiver, and I felt my body shaking, uncontrollably.

"Major... Major..." I couldn't get the words out.

"Oh, hell no!"

The ugly cry started, and it was over from there. I couldn't stop the tears or the snot from falling. Momma Peggy opened my door, rolled the window up, and killed the engine. She pulled me out of the car and hugged me. Wrapping my arms around her, I held on for dear life. If anyone knew my pain, this woman did.

She confided in me that Major's father cheated on her. The mistress actually showed up to their house and told her everything when he wouldn't leave his family for her. Not only did she have receipts, but she claimed to have had a child with him. That was when she packed up the kids and left.

I was the only person who knew the truth. Everyone else, including my husband and his brother, thought it was because of the way he treated her, so she let them believe that. During one of our talks, Momma Peggy said she blamed herself in the beginning. In her mind, she pushed him into this woman's arms. They always argued a lot and barely were intimate.

Momma Peggy said she had an idea he was stepping out on her. Even though her woman's intuition never steered her wrong, she decided not to confront him. All she wanted to do was survive the marriage until her kids graduated high school. Mr. Holland had financially crippled her, so she felt stuck.

Because he had enough respect for her to keep whoever it was a secret, Momma Peggy kept it pushing, until the disrespect met her head on. The woman confirmed the affair, which had been going on for nine years. She was someone he had met on a business trip in another state and moved the bitch to Jersey as their relationship progressed.

With me as her sounding board over the years, Momma Peggy had been able to finally heal from the hurt. Now, here I was about to stir up old emotions and memories for her.

"Talk to me, child. What did my son do?" Momma Peggy quizzed.

"Major cheated on me wit' our counselor," I blurted out.

"Let me get you inside before people start being nosey, and I have to cuss everyone out."

Once we entered the house, I went to the bathroom to clean

myself up. As I stared at the reflection in the mirror, my mind continued to race. I thought Major and I were good. This was the man who promised me forever. Why would he want to break me like this? Did he not care about how this would affect our children? When did the lines get blurred? How did I not see this coming? Why wasn't I enough?

After splashing some cold water on my face and blotting it dry with a hand towel, I slowly made my way to the kitchen.

"You good?" Momma Peggy inquired.

"No," I replied as the tears began to fall again.

I took a seat at the kitchen table. She was preparing the drink we also had whenever we got together, Malibu and pineapple with a splash of cranberry.

"Sip on this and tell me what happened." She handed me the beverage.

After finishing the drink in one swallow, I told Momma Peggy everything. She shook her head the entire time.

"I tried to call that son of mine, but he didn't answer. His ass has some explaining to do. I'm ready to go upside his mutha-fuckin' head." Her face was filled with rage. "Pull up the videos."

"You sure you wanna see it?" I questioned.

"Keep your hand over his shit. I just wanna see his damn face, so when he tries to lie to me and say it wasn't him, I can say I saw it for myself."

Momma Peggy looked at the videos, then slammed her fist on the table. It was the first time I viewed them all because my heart stopped at the first one when standing in the hotel. The video with her squatting over his face really fucked me up. I couldn't believe he would put the same lips he kisses our girls with on the pussy of another woman. It made me nauseous.

"This has me thinkin' she's not the first one. Now, every woman we know I question. Is he fuckin' the bitches he works wit'? Did he sleep wit' any of my friends? My mind won't rest until I get some answers. I wanna kill him. Like, for real. I know he's yo son, but that's how I feel."

"I just told his ass not too long ago that he was just like his father when it came to his thought process. Obviously, he acts like him too. I'm so sorry, Mecca. No one deserves this shit. We goin' back over to the hotel. Imma get his ass, you gone get her."

"But how? We don't even know what room he is in." I stared at her, confused.

"You're so upset, you can't even think clearly. Track his phone. If we have to bang on every damn door in that mutha-fucka, we will."

"Why the fuck didn't I think of that from the beginnin'?" I blew my breath.

"I'm glad you didn't. Things could have turned out worse than they already are. Let's get you some fighting clothes on 'cause that's a fuck me dress, and yo nasty ass probably don't have no drawers on." I smiled.

She always knew how to make a bad situation feel a lot better. Major definitely got that quality from her. Too bad all the qualities of his father showed up in him today.

Momma Peggy and I headed back to the hotel after I

changed. She drove this time. When I pulled up the app to track Major's phone, it was still showing it was at the hotel.

"I can't believe he's still there. He had to know by now I showed up and couldn't get access to the room. This shit is wild."

"Something is not adding up. For Major to say fuck you and his family out of the blue like this is crazy. If you didn't have those videos, it would be hard for me to believe he just switched up out of nowhere." She sighed.

When we finally arrived back at the hotel, Momma Peggy pulled into the no parking zone out front and parked anyway. We jumped out and went inside.

"Oh, no, she's back," I heard the guy who I was talking to earlier say when we approached the front desk.

"This is an emergency. My husband is up in one of your rooms and is in danger of losing his life," I explained. He was, though, so it wasn't a lie. "I tracked his phone, and it's showin' he's here. Unless you want me to call the police and have them clear this place out, you need to find out what room he is in."

When I showed him the tracker, he called over another worker. After I explained what happened, leaving out the cheating details, she hopped onto the computer.

"The manager helping you earlier quit on us, so I'm going to look up the rooms she checked-in today, since you claim she was supposed to be the one helping you. Do you have the name of the person who originally reserved the room?"

"Wanda Stevenson," I replied.

"I don't have that name in our system, but I do have one

under the name of the manager, which is odd. She shouldn't be reserving rooms while at work. Let me get the master key, and we can go check it out," she informed us.

"What's the odds of the lady quitting after you confronted her about the room? There's definitely some sneaky shit going on, and I don't like it." Momma Peggy kissed her teeth.

She worked for the IRS in the audit department and could detect some foul shit right away.

"The way she blacked out on me, I should have known her ass had somethin' to do wit' it. Why did she let him in and not me? Stupid bitch."

"Alright, follow me."

The covering manager led us up to the twenty-first floor. As we approached the room that was nestled in the corner, away from the elevators, my stomach started doing flips. I could feel the sweat forming on my brow.

When she unlocked the door, you could hear Major yelling for help. We rushed in and followed his voice. This muthafucka was still naked and handcuffed to the bed.

"Oh, damn, Son. I told you to go to counseling, not to hell and stay there."

"Why? Just tell me why?" I screamed and immediately jumped on the bed and started swinging. "You want yo dick sucked and pulled on? Well, let me help you out."

Before I could twist and snap his member from his body, Momma Peggy pulled me off of the bed by the back of the hoodie she gave me to wear as I kicked and screamed.

"Calm down." She had her arms wrapped around me.

"Not until I put my hands around that bitch's throat. Where is she, Major? Hiding in the closet?" I hollered.

"She's not here! Just let me explain what happened." He sounded just as defeated as I did.

"Can you please get me a towel to cover my son up and someone to cut him loose? Thank you."

Momma Peggy spoke to the woman who let us into the room. She went into the bathroom and came out with a towel, which she handed to me.

"I'll be right back with someone from maintenance." She turned on her heels and exited the room.

"Cover him up and let him explain what happened. If the shit ain't adding up, I'll kick his ass for you. Okay?" I shook my head yes.

There was nothing Major could say to get the image of Strawberry slobbing on his knob out of my head.

Chapter Thirteen

MAJOR

"Go ahead, lie to me."

Watching my wife glare at me with her arms folded across her chest, dressed like she was about to pull a lick, saddened me. Seeing my mom with her did lift my spirits some. If Mecca came up here by herself, I would have been left breathless for real, after she unalived my ass.

Hurt and disgust was written all over her face. Even though I was completely innocent in this situation, the damage had already been done. Like Strawberry said, the events of today would forever be etched in Mecca's mind.

"Nothing I'm 'bout to say is a lie. It's the absolute truth. Strawberry set our asses up. This was all part of some sick agenda she had planned out from the jump. I really thought she was you—"

"What the fuck you mean you thought she was me. See, now you 'bout to make me jump on yo ass again." Mecca pointed her finger toward my face.

"Son, you gotta do better than that. She's two seconds off yo ass, and I can't keep holding her strong ass back either. Mecca kicks like a mule." My mom always had jokes.

I explained everything that occurred from the moment I stepped foot in the room. The shit sounded crazy as hell. If I was Mecca, I would have a hard time believing the story I just told too.

"That's why she asked me what my favorite fragrance was and had me do this dumb as exercise with her. When she asked for the notes, she said it was because she wanted you to be ready when I showed up. I knew she was comin' up here, but she said to only decorate for us. I'm so fuckin' stupid." Mecca shook her head.

"Nah, this ain't on you or me. We had no reason not to trust her. And the reason you don't have the full video of me supposedly givin' her head is 'cause I tried to bite that mutha-fucka off once I realized it wasn't you. Look at the pillow. I spit the blood that was in my mouth out. Babe, you the only woman for me. There's not a female walkin' on this earth that can make me stray away from home. I got everything I need in you and our girls. Y'all my family." I started to get a little choked up.

I wasn't afraid to admit losing them was my biggest fear. Mecca was created for me. When I met her, I found my forever love, and our girls completed our circle. We had our own shit to deal with and needed to work on us, but there was never a moment where I ever thought of giving up on us.

"I'm back. The maintenance man is here to free him," the woman who was here earlier called out.

"Give us one minute," Momma Peggy yelled back. "Mecca, put his boxers on his ass."

Once I was decent, the man came into the room and cut the handcuffs off of me. I immediately jumped up to go hug Mecca.

"I love you, bruh." She started crying.

"I love you too, but Imma need you to wash yo mouth asap and shower, though." We laughed through the tears.

"I'm glad this shit ended on a good note 'cause damn. You had me scared for a moment, Son." My mom took a deep breath.

"It's not over yet. I need to lay hands and feet on Strawberry's ass," Mecca spewed.

"For tonight, it is. They need to give y'all a different room, since their worker had something to do with this shit, before I report all their asses. Order room service and try to enjoy this night the best y'all can."

"Nah, mom, we goin' home, and I don't wanna step foot in this bitch ever again."

I went into the bathroom to shower. The water was so hot, it felt like my skin was melting. I tried to scrub every trace of that ho off of me. When I got out, I brushed my teeth with the complimentary toothbrush and toothpaste they had on the bathroom counter for five minutes straight.

"Where everybody go?" I asked Mecca, after coming back into the bedroom fully dressed.

"They left. The manager apologized and offered us a free room at their sister hotel, and yo mom said she'll see us tomorrow when we go get my car. Do you think we should get the police involved?"

"Nah, we can handle this shit on our own. They wouldn't believe us no way or just say we got scammed." I grabbed my duffel bag, and we left.

The ride home was quiet as hell. Even though Mecca knew the truth, I understood she would still need some time to process it all. As soon as I opened my eyes tomorrow, I was calling my doctor to have a full workup done. I wanted to make sure I had a clean bill of health before I was intimate with Mecca again.

I still can't believe this crazy shit even happened. Strawberry, Wanda, or whoever the fuck she was definitely knew what the hell she was doing. She sucked us right in and played in our faces. For now, I had to concentrate on helping my wife mentally and emotionally heal from this, but I wasn't letting this shit go. Somehow, some way, I was going to get Strawberry's ass.

* * *

"Everything came back negative so far, but I will still recommend practicing safe sex until we run another round of tests in four weeks. I'll have my assistance schedule you an appointment."

My doctor advised me to wait two weeks before getting tested. He just called today with the results. I put him on speakerphone, so Mecca could hear it too.

"Thanks, Doc, we appreciate you. See you soon." I disconnected the call.

"Well, that's a relief. This was the longest two and half weeks of my life. Writin' in my journal has kept me sane."

"We gone get through this one day at a time."

I kissed Mecca on the forehead before getting up off the couch to go check on the girls. They were quiet as hell. It usually meant they were doing something they had no business.

"What did they tear up?" Mecca quizzed when I got back.

"Nothin', they fell asleep. It is their naptime." I sat back down.

"Did Savior find a new assistant yet? It's crazy how Dana's husband died during all of this. I guess movin' back home was the best thing for her. She's goin' to need all the support she can get, especially havin' young kids."

"He still doin' interviews. Well, I should say Sienna is." We laughed.

I never told Mecca about Dana because she would have told Sienna, and her ass would have lost it on my brother. When I told Savior, he had a hard time believing it, until her ass never showed back up at work. That was when he came up with the plan to tell our wives her husband died, since he never really existed anyway.

The picture on her desk of them was a fake. Savior took it out of the frame because it was the only picture he had of her. He wanted to save it to show these private investigators we planned on hiring. She had glued herself onto the picture that came with the frame. He said from a distance, the shit looked real.

After I told him what happened, we drove back over to the Breathless studio two days later, and the shit was already for rent. The owner was there showing people the space. He said the person who had been occupying it decided to terminate the lease early. When we asked what the person's name was, he said Foxy Brown. That was the name she signed the lease with when she paid for it in cash each year.

Since that was a dead end, we tried the counseling office. The office door was unlocked, and it had been completely empty. I don't know what type of operation Strawberry was running, but it had to be bigger than we imagined for her to clean house that fast.

"Since the kids will be sleep for the next hour, we can finally enjoy some adult time." Mecca smiled.

It had officially been five weeks since we indulged, and it was long overdue. Even though she was fucking crazy, everything Strawberry taught us wasn't. I scooped Mecca up and carried her into our room. We had a thirty-six pack of Magnum condoms waiting to be cracked open. It was time for me to leave her BREATHLESS.

. . .

Up Next... Breathless 2: Strawberry's Story

Author Charisse C. Carr Catalog:

***ovel***

A Romantic Entanglement Series
https://a.co/d/5bIsUhJ

Novellas

Valentine's Day With My Landlord
https://amzn.to/3OJxcbo
BCE: Beast Coast Entertainment: Diary Of A Secretary
https://amzn.to/3uLGFrt
Summer Luvin' With A Neighbor's Son
https://amzn.to/3zUw9A5
The Lake House: A Murder Mystery
https://amzn.to/41CfNcw
The Housewives of the Drug Game: Kalee & Bronx
https://bit.ly/410ETjA

A Billionaire's Christmas Wish
https://a.co/d/iZ6NuqB
Mutual Obsession
https://a.co/d/aI3hkdw
A Bully's Promise
https://a.co/d/gHfFe6M

Series

A Countdown To His Love
https://amzn.to/3CbVXJL
Harper & Stone: A Family Affair
https://bit.ly/442pD8f

Mali & Chaquille: A Dangerous Hood Love
https://amzn.to/3hQUf9i
Mali & Chaquille: A Dangerous Hood Love 2
https://amzn.to/3DlGBTD

The Asaad Brothers
https://a.co/d/7UxFfq8
The Asaad Brother: A Hitta's Revenge
https://a.co/d/2ufRR7O

A Billionaire's Dynasty: Rome Asaad's Story

https://a.co/d/cEHGfy1

Breathless

https://a.co/d/40FbH4i

Breathless 2

https://a.co/d/dayCOoR

Social Media:

Click on the link below to follow me on Facebook!

https://www.facebook.com/profile.php?id=100077944875169&mibextid=eHce3h

Click on the link below to follow me on Instagram!

https://www.instagram.com/authorcharisseccarr?igsh=Z3FtcWtwdjl6ZWt6&utm_source=qr

Click on the link below to follow me on TikTok!

https://www.tiktok.com/@authorcharisseccarr?_t=8ibAddJaArz&_r=1

Made in the USA
Middletown, DE
16 November 2024